The Antarean Odyssey is about the birth of a peo___ ___ the fiery end of their home-world. It is a story about adventure, love, heartbreak, sorrow, and of overcoming difficult and often dangerous situations.

The Antarean Odyssey
Book One
The Labors of Jonathan

One evening Jonathan Wright overhears a conversation about a world wide cartel, an interstellar trade agreement, and aliens called Altruscans.

The Antarean Odyssey
Book Two
The Original Four

Book two is about four girls coming from diverse cultures and backgrounds, and they are the beginning of the Antarean people.

The Antarean Odyssey
Book Three
Loss of Eden

The ending of childhood might feel like the loss of Eden. It is time for the four to meet the world. The story is about an expedition that goes terribly wrong. Sabrina races home against time and death only to find a deserted ship. The Antares is only manned by androids.

The Antarean Odyssey
Book Four
Starship Trefayne

Sabrina didn't mind leaving Acheron. But she was not too crazy about having to drop her studies and then, being a guinea pig integrating a Chiron starship.

If Captain Thalon, aka, Sargon, thought to have Sabrina safely on the Trefayne, he will soon learn otherwise.

The Antarean Odyssey
Book Five
Misalliance

Now is the time for Commander Sarah Thalon, Chief Medical Officer of the Worldship Antares to leave home to become an intern on Madras to fulfill a requirement of Starfleet of the Planetary Alliance

Books to be published are

The Antarean Odyssey
Assignment Earth
Book Six

The Antarean Odyssey
Matched
Book Seven

The Antarean Odyssey
Misalliance
Inge Blanton

The Antarean Odyssey
Misalliance

Inge Blanton

iUniverse, Inc.
New York Bloomington

The Antarean Odyssey
Misalliance

Copyright © 2010 Inge Blanton

This is a work of fiction. All of the characters, names, incidents, organizations, and dialogue in this novel are either the products of the author's imagination or are used fictitiously.

iUniverse books may be ordered through booksellers or by contacting:

iUniverse
1663 Liberty Drive
Bloomington, IN 47403
www.iuniverse.com
1-800-Authors (1-800-288-4677)

ISBN: 978-1-4502-3671-3 (pbk)
ISBN: 978-1-4502-3670-6 (ebk)

Printed in the United States of America

iUniverse rev. date: 8/16/2010

Chapter 1

There was a broad smile and pure enjoyment written all over Sarah's face as she looked eagerly around to satisfy her curiosity. High-rises and cars indeed she thought, just like back on Earth. The planet Madras reminded her of how things used to look on Earth. Also, it had been such a long time since she'd seen so many people in one place. She had no idea that humanoids came in such a variety of sizes, shapes and colors. She and Sargon just finished going through formalities and exited the Port of Entry. The day was sunny and bright. It was a beautiful spring day

If it wasn't for being forced to leave home, I could really enjoy all this, Sarah thought. It was a never before experienced treat to be somewhere where she could see people. Until now, whenever she had been away from the Antares, it was on a small island in the middle of an ocean. She turned her face toward the sun, the warmth felt good. Taking a deep breath, she slowly let it out.

Sargon standing beside her, smiled

Sarah, seeing the smile, looked narrowly at him, then, asked, "What are you grinning about?"

"You. You're doing what everybody does when coming off ship." Amused at her questioning look, he added, "They take a deep whiff of fresh air."

Sarah scowled and tried to ignore the grin. "Well, what are we waiting for?" she wanted to know, realizing they were still standing outside the Port of Entry.

"We are waiting for a courtesy car from the hospital. We are supposed to be picked up… just about now," Sargon said, and pointed to an air-cab that was in the process of landing. On its side, very visible, was the hospital's logo.

"You know, what I really like, is to go back home," Sarah said apprehensively, and pulled a face.

"I understand, but believe me, there's much for you to look forward to and, to learn. For the first time, you will have people and real cases to work with."

"Yes I know, but I'm still scared."

"You will get over it."

She gave Sargon a morose look, thinking that's easy for you to say when it is me who has to do it.

Sargon read her emotions and gave her an encouraging pat, then handed her into the car.

Port City, built on a peninsula jutting out into the ocean, was a self-contained community. There was the Space Port, the hospital, then the many consulates from different planets with homes to house their personnel; also Star Fleet headquarters with its staff. There were hotels, shops, some elegant, some not so fancy. It had night clubs and theaters. Port City also had a seedy side. Visiting Sikar, the city proper, was discouraged. The Madrians hemmed about societal differences which could produce culture shock. What they didn't voice was the fear of having their superior culture diluted or changed by alien influences.

From the air, the hospital appeared to be an enormous complex, spread over several acres. When they landed, the car was met by the hospital's administrator.

"Captain Thalon, Miss Thalon, welcome to Madras, and especially to the Academy Hospital. I'm Argelus, the hospital's administrator. Miss Thalon, we are happy to have you. I have seen some of your test scores and, we are impressed. Please, let me give you a tour, and then my secretary can show you to your apartment."

As they entered the building, they were met by one of Mister Argelus's aides. "Sir, I'm sorry, but there is an urgent call for you." Turning to Sargon, "I can conduct the tour, if you don't mind."

Sargon knew it to be fiction. For the first time he had an inkling that everything was not as it had been advertised. There had been no such call. It had never been the administrator's intention of giving them the tour. It had all been a act.

The tour given by the aid covered a succession of emergency rooms, then the imaging center. Sarah was particularly interested in the Magnetic Resonance Imaging Scanner. Then they were shown to the radiotherapy building and the new neonatal unit. Also, the hospital was famous for its extensive rehabilitation facility. Even Sargon was impressed.

After the tour, they were courteously handed over to a secretary. She made a deep obeisance to Sargon. "Let me show you the apartment," she said in a low, depreciative voice.

Sarah's assigned apartment was in a building stowed away in an isolated corner of the hospital's ground. When Sargon gave the secretary a surprised look, she said apologetically, "We have so few female interns." And to Sarah, "I didn't think you would find it comfortable sharing a dorm with our male interns."

Sarah's apartment was in a three storied house, surrounded by huge trees. It was small and dingy looking with a minuscule kitchen and a cramped living room. It had one bedroom with a private bath. The furniture looked to be second-hand.

Sargon was very dissatisfied. The brochure had promised adequate housing and the best facilities. On his first tour with Ian McPherson, they were shown just that. It slowly dawned on him that this was for males only. Ian had enjoyed his stay on Madras, and gave a glowing description.

Before he left, Sargon gave Sarah a code, assuring her it would reach him anywhere if she ever needed him. Also, if she ever required legal advice, she was to contact the embassy of Acheron. They had been informed of her stay here.

* * *

Sarah found the medical establishment to be ultra modern, outfitted with the best and newest equipment, and the wards were sunny and bright. Everything was done to make the patient comfortable. To reach the hospital from the women's housing, she had to enter through a back gate. It took fifteen minutes to make her way to the hospital and then, down the main staircase to the demonstration room where she attended her first teaching session of the day. The class was small, consisting mainly of outworlders; the language was Galactic.

At their first session, the students were introduced to their principal instructor, the senior surgeon. His name was Galus, and he too came from another world. His first lecture was on the differences in alien anatomies.

The second instructor was a woman Sarah guessed to be Madrian. She gave most of her attention to the men, and virtually ignored the women in her class. Her lecture was given in a low voice. She looked as though she might easily simper, and Sarah felt little patience for her.

Sarah was to spend her mornings in the classrooms with instructors, and in the afternoon, made rounds through the wards. Her first day ended with the last round late that night. Her face was drawn and she was utterly exhausted when she fell into her bed.

* * *

Early the next morning she was awakened by a violent storm, with winds of varying intensity. The great trees around the house creaked and groaned under the onslaught. Sarah stood by the window and looked out in dismay. The rain came down in sheets. She had no raincoat. How would she make it to the hospital?

As if an answer to her prayer, Lanei, a second year intern she'd met yesterday, put her head through the door and said, "I could give you a lift if you don't mind piling into my car." Lanei had been very helpful explaining procedures and how to read and keep charts all through yesterday's rounds.

"I'm very happy to take your offer. I was just trying to figure out how I would get myself to the hospital without getting soaked."

Sarah squeezed into the car already filled to capacity. When they arrived at the hospital, they were immediately herded into a van to be taken to Sikar's community hospital. The storm had caused a train derailment and all the city's emergency rooms were full of injured people.

The chief surgeon from the community hospital arrived just as the van from Port City drove up. He waved for them to follow him to the emergency rooms. In the emergency room, Sarah, walking behind him, was amused as he tut-tutted over every injury before beginning his examination.

"Anyone familiar with triage?"

"I am, sir," Sarah informed him.

"Okay, go to it," he told her.

For most of the morning, Sarah worked in sorting the most severely injured from the ones who could survive with first aid. Later on, she assisted the chief surgeon who had been called in from the Academy Hospital, whose name was Miles, in surgery.

"You'd make a good nurse," he complimented her.

"Doctor Miles, I'm a physician from the Worldship Antares. Up to now I've had very little opportunity to study alien anatomy. This is the reason I'm here on Madras."

He looked up quickly. "Meaning, the Madrians are aliens?"

"Precisely."

He digested this for a moment. "Okay, Doc..." he said, squinting at her name tag, "Thalon, would you be interested in studying surgery?"

"Very."

"I can't promise anything, but I'll see what I can do."

* * *

Sarah hoped something would come of Doctor Miles offer, but spring passed into summer, and she still hadn't heard from him. At least she had made friends. There were three women from other worlds interning just like her. They had banded together as a study group and for mutual encouragement, and also out of loneliness.

The work was arduous and the hours long. There was very little free time. To their surprise by the years end they were joined by Ogden, the only Madrian who seemed to show a friendly disposition toward them. Ogden was in the last year of his internship and had lived most of his life in Port City.

One morning, when exiting the apartment complex with Lanei, Sarah stopped and gasped. Where has the year gone to? she thought. She had come to Madras in the spring, and now it was snowing. She held out her hands to catch the flakes.

"You've never seen snow?" Lanei asked.

"Oh yes, but that was a long time ago."

"The winters here are usually mild. I'm surprised it is snowing. Can you get away for the winter solstice? There's an island farther south. We could stay at a beach there."

"The Madrian's don't object?"

"Oh, the island is frequented mostly by Alliance personnel like Ambassadors, starship captains, etcetera, and very few Madrian's."

* * *

In her second year, Sarah joined the School of Pediatrics. The atmosphere was much more relaxed, although the hours were just as demanding. She met Silvan, who later turned out to be Ogden's girlfriend. Silvan was studying to become a pediatrician.

Silvan was only part Madrian and most of her friends were outworlders, as the Madrians called them. Her father worked in the Admiralty of the Alliances' Fleet as an administrator.

After nearly a year in the pediatric unit, Sarah was asked if she would like to work in Sikar's children's hospital. Of course she agreed. Every morning she was picked up by a van and taken to the hospital, and every evening she was deposited in front of her apartment. She was given no time, or opportunity, to go sight-seeing into Sikar. Even her lunch had to be eaten in the hospital's cafeteria.

After she had been at the hospital for several months, Sarah discovered a special ward with five little wide eyed girls who gave her a bright smile whenever she entered their room. One morning, before starting her rounds, she went to check on one of the girls who had seemed restless the night before. When she entered the room, the bed was empty. The nurse told her that the girl had died during the night.

"But she wasn't that ill," Sarah responded.

"Things like that happen. Sometimes you think they are getting better and then, they suddenly die on you."

"I'd like to see her chart," Sarah told the nurse.

"Doctor Ravan has it and I doubt if he will let you see it."

The nurse was right he didn't let her see the chart. He told her that it was none of her business, and that she should attend to the patients assigned to her. After that, the room with the little girls was off limits to her. It wasn't the sudden death of the girl that first roused Sarah's suspicions, but the doctor and nurse's attitude. They seemed to write the girl's death off as a minor incident.

Later, at her apartment, she phoned Silvan and told her about it.

"Could you manage to get assigned to the hospital?" Sarah asked her.

"Probably not. You think something weird is going on there?"

"Well, I don't know how to put it. There are four remaining girls. I slipped in one day and examined them. Nothing appeared to be wrong. They receive medications that make no sense, so I took blood samples. I have the slides in my purse. Could you do some tests for me?"

"What do you suspect?"

"I don't want to say anything right now. I also wrote down the medication they are giving those kids."

* * *

The next morning, before starting her rounds, Sarah looked in on the girls. She moved silently across the darkened room and approached the crib with the smallest girl in it. To her surprise, Sarah saw the child under a plastic oxygen tent. Her eyes were closed with a tape and ointment oozed from underneath it. Sarah moved the plastic aside and when she bent over her, she could hear the breathing was shallow. At a closer look, the child's face was gray.

Sarah pressed the emergency button. When the nurse came in, she pointed to the girl and asked, "What has happened?"

"Her pneumonia is not responding to treatment."

"But she did not have pneumonia yesterday," Sarah said angrily.

"Doctor Ravan diagnosed her with pneumonia when she was admitted," the nurse answered, unruffled.

Sarah wiped the perspiration from her forehead and felt like she was about to explode. She was stunned. There is something wrong in this hospital she thought. She turned and quickly left the room before someone asked inopportune questions. She was determined to investigate. Later in the afternoon, she was called into Doctor Ravan's office.

"Miss Thalon, the nurse in ward six has told me that you are interfering with her duty," he said sternly.

"What duty?"

His thin face tightened and he looked resentfully at Sarah. "Don't you get impertinent with me, young lady!"

"I'm not impertinent, only very curious. I was told that the youngest girl in ward six has pneumonia. I saw her yesterday and she seemed all right."

"Are you a physician?"

Sarah kept the dislike out of her voice with extreme difficulty. "It might surprise you, but I am."

"Then, what are you doing here?"

"A requirement of the Alliance Charter decrees that to be a doctor in Space Fleet you have to have a diploma from one of their accredited medical facilities. I'm here to get certified."

"I see." Ravan rose to his feet, and his face tightened. "Thank you, Miss Thalon, I will look into the situation."

"And you will inform me?"

"When I find something to report."

Three days later, against her protest, Sarah was dismissed. A week later, she was reassigned to the surgical department back in Port City

Chapter 2

On her first day back at the Port City hospital, Sarah was to report to the chief surgeon. Mustering all her composure, she entered his office.

He looked her over as she stood in front of his desk. "So, you're interested in surgery. Doctor Miles has spoken to me about you. Have you done any dissecting?"

"Yes."

Pointing to a chair, he said, "Please sit down, I have a few forms for you to fill out." When the paperwork was completed and a few rules explained, she was instructed to come back in two days.

Sarah spent the two days becoming familiar with the surgical department, and buying the books she would need. She ran into Ogden as she came out of the bookstore.

"Sarah! What are you doing here?"

"I'm now in the surgical department."

"I thought you were working in Sikar's Children's Hospital."

She stepped closer and whispered conspiratorially into his ear, "They didn't like me being there. They thought me too nosey."

Ogden gave her an amused look. Then more serious, "Silvan talked to me about it. Like you, she's intrigued. She's almost finished with the tests."

"Oh good, tell her to come to see me once they're completed."

Instead of coming to see Sarah during the weekend, Silvan invited her to her parent's home. Sarah ascended the stairs and was about to knock when the door was opened by a stiff and very pompous looking individual. He had a supercilious face and looked down his long nose at her. "May I help you, Miss?"

Sarah had never met a butler, but knew from old movies who or what he was. Still, she was so nonplussed, she stared speechlessly at him. She had to collect herself before she could say, "I'm Sarah Thalon to see Silvan."

"Xantho, will you please announce Lady Sarah to Silvan," Ogden said with a chuckle as he came up behind the butler.

"Very well, Sir," Xantho said unbending, and walked stiffly away.

"I'm sorry Sarah. I was supposed to have picked you up. When I went to your place, you were already gone."

"That's a butler?" Sarah asked awed, pointing to the retreating back.

"He does look formidable," Ogden agreed, looking amused.

Silvan came from somewhere in the back of the house. She gave Ogden a wave of her hand and then looked at Sarah. "Hello Sarah, come in. My father would like to meet you."

"Your father?"

"I gave the report to him."

"I wish you hadn't, Silvan."

She led Sarah to a huge double door and opened it with a flourish. "Father, may I introduce my friend, Sarah?"

Silvan's father sat at his desk with papers spread in front of him. At first, he only glanced up, then, slowly rose. From Silvan's description of Sarah, he had expected someone totally different. Sarah looked to be about Silvan's age, but her carriage and poise let him suspect that she was not a young impressionable girl.

"Lady Sarah, he said, "would you please be seated?"

Sarah was somewhat chilled by his cold, probing eyes. Silvan's bubbly personality had led her to expect someone very different. Also, since he was an administrator in the Admiralty, he may decide to bring this matter to the attention of the proper authority, for which she was not yet ready.

"Thank you. I had no intention of troubling you. I thought to give Silvan a short visit. Mister…"

"I'm sorry, my name is Algoron."

"Mister Algoron, I only came to get a report Silvan was working on for me."

"Yes, Silvan showed it to me."

He handed Sarah a folder he took from his desk drawer. Sarah opened it, and leafed through, then astonished looked at Algoron. It was severely abbreviated. It only showed the girls blood types and the reason the medication was given. Sarah slowly rose. "Mister Algoron, let me introduce myself. I'm Commander Sarah Thalon, Chief Medical officer of the Worldship Antares. I might sound like a broken record, but let me reiterate, I am only here because I need a certificate from an accredited medical facility." She pointed to the folder. "This report might fool a child," she said icily. Then, standing ramrod straight, she bowed and turned toward the door.

"Commander Thalon." his voice was ironic as he addressed her. "What was the purpose of this report?"

"Only to satisfy my curiosity. Good day, Mister Algoron." She walked past Silvan and Ogden and out of the house.

After Sarah left, Algoron rose and went out of the room for a minute. When he returned, he sat down heavily in his chair. "Silvan, I don't want you to associate too much with this lady. That goes for you too, Ogden."

"Would you mind telling me why?" Ogden asked.

"This report could be very damaging to certain people."

Ogden's eyebrows went up. "Will you use it?"

Algoron only shrugged his shoulders.

* * *

Sarah noticed that she was being followed. Instead of going straight to the Embassy of Acheron as she had intended, she changed direction and headed home. She had never been so angry and was determined not to be thwarted. She resolved to get the result of her inquiry one way or another.

Next evening, there was a knock on her door and Sarah was startled to see Ogden. "You surprise me. I would have wagered that Algoron forbade you to see me."

"Oh, not quite forbidden, but warned me that you're not what you seem to be."

"Yes, I expected that. Especially after he had me followed."

"Oh, he did that? I wondered why he left the room. I came to say hi from Silvan, and to tell you that she will give you the report once she gets her hands on it. The findings troubled her too, so, she wants to get at the bottom of it. I'm also here to extend an invitation. It snowed for several nights in the mountains." He was interrupted by the slam of the door as Silvan came racing up the stairs.

Breathlessly she uttered, "Did you ask her?"

"I was just about to do that when you interrupted." Turning back to Sarah he asked, "What are you going to do during the holidays?"

"Work. I'm taking care of an old man who hasn't improved since he came out of surgery."

"If you can, we'd like for you to join us. We're going up to my father's ski lodge," Silvan told her. "Do you ski?" she asked as an afterthought.

"Of course. It would be a nice break. Tell me, there's a rumor floating around that you two are going to get married?"

"Only if he promises to live in Port City."

"You don't like Sikar?" Sarah asked, surprised.

"It's not Sikar. I'm just used to Port City's culture. My mother's relatives live in Sikar and they are very restrictive. You see, my mother is Madrian. Sometimes I have to go and visit them, but I stay as briefly as possible. They don't like the way I dress, or the way I talk. Mostly, they would like to marry me off to someone else since they don't think Ogden is a suitable choice. My father promised that I could marry whoever I choose; naturally with his approval and he seems to like Ogden."

"That would help," Sarah said, smiling at Silvan.

"Do you like it here?"

"No Silvan. I'd rather go home, but I'm advised to stay and finish my residency."

"Do you have family?"

Sarah looked at her pensively and slowly said, "Yes and no. I have family, but not as you understand it, and the relationships are difficult to explain."

Silvan looked at Sarah but thought to defer finding out what that enigmatic statement meant and instead said, "Sarah, I didn't like what the report showed. Let's talk it over at the new tea-room that opened down Galaxy's way."

* * *

Sarah found it increasingly difficult to concentrate on her patient's problems. The report had disturbed her, as well as Silvan's warning that she could be stirring up a hornet's nest. Recently, she's been given the care of an old man whose symptoms worsened. Sarah ordered a battery of tests and now was waiting for the results, and they would not arrive until later that evening. She just couldn't leave him. He was a grouchy old man, and often abrasive, but she had developed a fondness for him.

When the results came in, her fears were confirmed. He had leukemia. In two days, Silvan and friends would go up to the ski lodge, but Sarah felt like she couldn't leave the old man for such a frivolous pursuit. When she came to work the next morning, she was informed that his case had been transferred to a more experienced doctor. She didn't know if she should be mad, or relieved. When she saw Ogden that afternoon, she told him angrily that she felt belittled when her patient was assigned to someone else.

"They took the old man away from you?" he asked, understanding her anger.

"Yes. Naturally, they preferred Doctor Ray, the ninny, over me, because he's a male." Sarah's patience was often severely strained by the condescending attitudes the Madrian's showed toward women. She told Ogden that she would accept their invitation to have a holiday.

* * *

On that ski trip, Sarah befriended a distant cousin of Ogden named Meshab Ashlan. When he turned up in the surgical department during her fourth year on Madras, she was pleased. Meshab was full of laughter and he had an easy going manner. He was pleasant to be around and easy to make friends with. When Ogden tried to discourage her growing friendship with Meshab, Sarah couldn't understand why. When she asked, he became evasive.

Sarah and Meshab often worked closely together. They followed the same doctors through the wards and saw the same patients. Meshab often reminded her of Peter, the little brother she had raised. As far as Sarah was concerned, they were good friends. When he asked if he could compare his notes with hers, she didn't mind, and she sometimes helped edit his papers.

Late one evening, disheartened and exhausted, she dragged herself to the dining hall to get a bit to eat before going home. She had been working all day trying to save a man who had third degree burns over eighty percent of his body. The effort had proven futile. She was just about to sit down, when Meshab approached her.

"You look awful," he said.

"I feel awful," Sarah told him. "My patient didn't make it."

Meshab bit his lip. "I heard you are off for the next two days. You need a break. Would you like to go out with me tomorrow evening, around seven?"

"That would be nice. Are Ogden and Silvan coming? I know Ogden is off and he said something about going out to dinner."

"No, he didn't say anything to me. I guess they are making it a twosome. It would only be you and me. Would you like that?" There was an infectious bright smile on his face to which Sarah responded with a smile of her own.

"I guess so," she told him. "Where are we going?"

"Let that be a surprise."

"Then I will see you tomorrow evening at seven."

"Thank you, gracious lady," he teased, and he gave her a smile she could not read. But he seemed to be genuinely pleased.

She had been asked to go on a date. Sarah was astonished. Someone had really asked her. Maybe she was going to have a social life after all.

* * *

Meshab was punctual. When she answered the knock at her door, he stood several steps back holding a bunch of flowers. His face changed from a nonchalant expression to a look of admiration. Sarah was tall, slender and had enormous black eyes. The bright colors of her gown complemented her dark complexion, and her hair was combed away from her face into a chignon at the back of her neck.

"You are beautiful," he told her, and offered the bouquet.

No one had ever called her beautiful. Unconsciously, her hand brushed over her gown and she stood a little straighter. She gave him a dazzling smile. "You are very gracious, and thank you for the flowers."

First thing on the agenda was to dine at an elegant restaurant. The waiters were very solicitous and spoke in subdued voices. It was the most fashionable eating place in Port City, almost exclusively frequented by off-worlders. Sarah found the food exotic and delicious, although the wine he ordered was heady.

It was so easy to relax in Meshab's company. He was urbane, witty, and she enjoyed his company immensely. Their conversation was mostly on the light side, but at times his comments became suggestive. When she failed to demur, there was a slightly indulgent smile on his face.

Later on, he aroused her curiosity by describing a very popular night club. He tried to convince her to come with him. At first she wasn't sure she wanted to go; her head wasn't too clear. She had drunk only a little of the wine, but its effect was clouding her judgment. He was persistent and she finally gave in.

They walked together arm in arm, laughing and talking, just a few buildings down. Inside the club, the lights were multi colored and dim, and she could see dancers swaying to the enticing rhythm of soft music. Enchanted, Sarah gave a gasp of surprise. There was a small table waiting for them. Meshab ordered a drink and then asked her to dance. As they floated and swirled around the dance floor, he kissed her and told her she was the most bewitching woman he had ever met.

It was way past midnight when he called a cab. They arrived at her apartment and she gave him the key to unlock the door because she felt a bit unsteady.

"Meshab," she told him, "this was a most enjoyable evening. Will I see you tomorrow?"

Instead of leaving, he began kissing her again, deep and long. She felt her body responding to him and her arms went around his neck to hold him close.

* * *

Sarah awoke next day, tired and heavy headed. It was already past noon and the place beside her bed was empty. She wondered if it had just been a dream. Her head was throbbing; must be a hangover she thought. After dressing, she dragged herself to the dining hall. Ogden came to her table. "Sarah, what happened? You look awful."

"I feel awful. I think I have a hangover. I never had one before in my whole life. Is there something you can do about it?"

"I'll get you something." When he reappeared, he gave her a glass of some red looking liquid. "Drink this; it should help in a few minutes." He sat down and looked searchingly at her. "Now tell me what happened."

She told him about the most marvelous evening she had ever spent, dining and dancing. She also told him that she had slept with Meshab. Looking at him with her big, black eyes in wonder she said, "You know, I think I'm in love with him, and I think he loves me too." Her face was bright with happiness.

Ogden's face remained serious. "Sarah," he said, "I hope he loves you too." He rose swiftly and there was hardness in his eyes. She misunderstood his behavior, thinking she had violated his moral standard.

When Sarah arrived at the hospital the next morning, she looked for Meshab, but he was not on her morning round. It was Ogden who had taken his place. When she asked him later, he told her that Meshab had asked to be reassigned to another section of the hospital.

"But why?"

"You need to ask him yourself…"

"I don't allow private conversations on my rounds," the lecturing physician reprimanded them.

After making rounds, she went to the dining hall but found neither Ogden nor Meshab. She brought a journal to read but soon became aware of the stares and whispers. They stopped at once when she looked up. During the afternoon lectures, she found all the seats taken and nobody was willing to make room for her. She found a spare seat against the far wall and wondered what was going on. As she finished her rounds that evening, one of the interns came up to her and pinched her on the bottom. Sarah grabbed his wrist and bent it backward, saying levelly, "Don't ever do that again."

The next day, it was the same thing again. She was jostled and no one would make room for her to sit down. She could see the leers and hear the whispers. By evening, disgusted and totally confused, she retired to her apartment to study. Before she went to bed, there was a light tap on her door. When she opened it, Silvan asked if she could come in.

"Of course, Silvan. Are you by yourself?"

"Ogden couldn't come, but he knows I'm here."

"What's going on?"

"Sarah, Ogden tried to warn you not to get to friendly with Meshab."

"I know. I should have listened."

"Yes but. I think you don't understand. Meshab made a bet that he could bed you any time he chose. He is not in love with you. He is engaged to be married as soon as he graduates."

Sarah turned ashen and her hands flew to her face. Then she felt herself turn red in the face. She gave Silvan a stricken look. "I must be the world's greatest fool," she said hoarsely.

"Ogden said Meshab made you drunk."

Sarah closed her eyes to avoid looking at Silvan. "Yes, I was drunk. And I should have known better. I believed him. I trusted him. We worked side by side all these months. I've watched how he cared for his patients. Oh, I don't know. Thank you for coming."

Sarah, I'm only half Madrian. My father, as you know, is from another world. When I asked him what to do, he told me that the kindest thing was to warn you. But I was too late."

"Thank you Silvan, and if Ogden doesn't want to be seen with me, I'll understand."

"Maybe not for a while, but he understands and knows that you were deceived."

"Tell him I appreciate his kind thoughts. Please Silvan, I need to be alone."

"I understand."

When Silvan left, Sarah stood motionless for a long time looking out of the window.

* * *

The next days were a rerun of those preceding. Toward the end of one her shifts, she was unexpectedly pushed through an open door. She felt the hot breath of a male against her ear as he tried to have her hand touch his genitals.

Sarah's anger surged. She could feel the blood rushing to her face as she pushed him away. "Darren!" she said through clenched teeth, "stop this, or you will regret it."

"Ah you little whore, don't fight what you so obviously enjoy," he said genially. "Just a little body touching and then I'll let you go."

Sarah grabbed his hand and squeezed it tight until he grunted. When he tried to push her to the floor, she hauled out and her fist landed in his face. He let out a howl and slung at Sarah with his open hand. She parried it with her arm and hit him again. He rocked back and glared at her. Sarah felt a shiver of fear.

"You will regret this, whore," he said as he backed out and closed the door.

For the next several days nothing happened, and Sarah began to let her guard down. Suddenly the notes from her class disappeared and a week later, someone destroyed her books. Her test papers were getting misplaced. Then one day she came home to find her apartment vandalized. She thought if this keeps up, I'm going to make sure I have evidence. First, she called the police, then, took pictures of the destruction. Now at least there would be an official report of her complaint.

The next day she made an appointment with the dean. The dean listened to her with great courtesy and told her that he would have someone look into it. Then she was politely eased out of the door.

When Sarah left the dean's office, she set out at a brisk walk. Yeah sure, he would do something about it. More likely, it would be swept under the rug, she fumed. Her intention was to stop by the embassy, but it was already closed. She was tired but less angry when she returned home. On her computer she discovered two communiqués. One was an open letter from Sargon giving her the date and time he would be in Port City. The second one was from Ayhlean. It was in two parts and scrambled. As she unscrambled Ayhlean's letter, written on the very top was the instruction to read Kamila's letter first. Sarah read it twice to make sure she understood, then, began to laugh. Oh that devious Kamila, she thought, then gave a triumphant shout, "She did it!" The second letter was gossip from the space station, and all the latest news about Sabrina, and all the goings on in Ayhlean's life. Written on the bottom in big letters and underlined twice was, "Kamila is pregnant!!!"

Chapter 3

Four days later, Sarah met Sargon at the Port of Entry. He was dressed in the Antarean uniform and only carried a small bag. Her eyes lit up with pleasure while he smiled indulgently at her.

"I missed you," were the first words out of her mouth.

"I'm very happy to see you too," he said. "Mind if we walk?" he asked. "The weather is too nice not to enjoy, and I have been cooped up in the ship too long."

"How long can you stay?" she asked him.

"I only have an overnight layover."

"You have a place to stay?"

"No."

"You could stay at my place."

"Don't you think it would be a little bit crowded?"

"I could make room."

By the time they arrived at Sarah's apartment, she had shared with him all the news about Ayhlean's letter, and about Kamila's. Holding the keys in her hand, Sarah met his eyes squarely and asked;" Don't you have anything to say?"

There was no comment, only a smile as he took the keys from her and opened the door. Once inside her tiny living room, Sargon turned toward her. "Now tell me how are you doing? How are your studies coming along?" He reached out and gently touched her cheek. It was like a shock. Startled, he pulled back. "Sarah, what has happened? I'm getting an impression of very disturbed emotional feelings from you," he told her.

Sarah sighed. "Please, just sit down." She wanted to compose herself first.

"Let me make some coffee," and went into the kitchenette. He followed and settled himself on top of the small table. "Sarah, something happened?"

"Let's talk over a cup of coffee." She tried to postpone what she feared would be an embarrassing disclosure. After the coffee was brewed, she gave him a cup.

He wrapped his hands around it and said, "Now, quit stalling."

She looked at him with chagrin and squirmed, "I don't know how to tell you."

"Well, start at the beginning."

"I lost my virginity," she blurted out, wishing she were dead.

In all his life, Sargon had never been so nonplussed. Leaning back, he looked speechlessly at her. "You lost what?"

"You heard me," she said, and began to cry.

Sargon put his cup down and came around the table to pull her up from the chair. He lifted her chin and made her look at him. "Come Sarah, tell me what happened."

She began haltingly at first, then, went into all the details of her ordeal. When she finished, she said, "I hate myself for being so stupid."

"Sarah," Sargon said, as he took her hands in his, and gave them a gentle squeeze. "Trusting someone needs no excuse. How could you have known?" When her tears began to flow, he embraced her. Suddenly, he was plunged into her agonizing memories, first her initial bewilderment, and then her self-disdain. He was totally taken off guard when her lips fastened on to his mouth and she passionately kissed him. Scanning, he realized she was asking for his acceptance of her. Gently he returned her kisses.

She looked timidly up into his face, finding only kindness, understanding, and acceptance. Her tears were still flowing freely down her cheeks, but a smile soon lit up her face. "Do you love me?" she asked.

"Yes, I love you. I always have."

She moved a little closer and found herself uncomfortable under his gaze. "Always?" she asked. "No promises?"

"No Sarah, no promises."

"But house-rights?"

"Is that what you are asking?"

"What I am asking of you, you can't or won't give. Oh Jim...I," then she gave up. "Do you know your shirt is wet?" she said matter of fact, and began to unbutton it.

"Now, Sarah ..."

"You can't walk around with a tear-stained shirt," she interrupted.

With a sigh, he gave in and handed her his shirt. She went into the bathroom and washed it out in the basin. When she came back, he was standing at the window, looking out. When she joined him, he pointed, "Someone's interested in what you're doing."

"I know. I have been maligned, called a whore, and stalked."

He turned toward her and said, "You need not stay here. Tell me if you want to leave."

"Yes. I'm not very happy here, and I doubt the persecutions will stop."

"You think you could hold the fort for another three months?"

"Yes, if I can see an end in sight. Then it won't matter what they think of me."

"What they think of you won't matter. What you think of yourself does," he told her sternly. "Remember the onus is always on the deceiver. You gave him your trust. He is a liar, remember that."

She stood so close, she could feel the warmth of his body, and as much as she tried to fight it, her senses responded to him. "It matters what you think of me," she told him.

Sargon drew Sarah close, and as his arm went around her, her head came to rest against his chest. Holding her, he said "Sarah, you are lovely and you are beautiful, and ..." Whatever else he was going to say was smothered by her mouth. As he loosened her hair, her hands moved up his chest, then to his neck, and her body pressed close to his.

Later as they lay resting, he tried to fight the lassitude and the need to sleep. Her face was buried in his neck and she was still breathing hard. "Sarah?" When she lifted her face to him, he gently kissed her on the lips, then, asked, "Do you still remember how to meditate?"

"You want to go into meditation?" she asked, incredulous.

Sargon laughed. "No silly," he said. "You have been hurt. A healing is necessary, so don't argue. Also, should you become pregnant you need to know how to bond with your baby. It's the same technique. After you do this, you will always know where your child is, and what its needs are. You will always be in contact with it. So, pay close attention to how it's done."

"Yes Sir," she said and smiled up at him.

"Okay, now do it."

She felt no apprehension as he guided her into a meditative state. Sargon was never intrusive. She could feel his gentle thoughts, his love and caring, and that he perceived her as beautiful, gentle and intelligent. Then he gave her a picture that was his favorite memory of her. She could see herself as a tall, skinny, young girl with big eyes and a sulky expression. He let her feel what this impetuous thirteen year old had meant to him. When she came out of meditation she asked, "Did I really look like that waif I've seen in your mind?"

"Yes. You and Sabrina, you were my two biggest hoydens." Then he laughed and pulled her into his arms again.

* * *

Sargon met her next morning in study hall, wearing his Antarean uniform and dark glasses.

"Good morning, Sarah," he said, and stopped at her table strewn with books, journals and notebooks. He picked up one of the books and leafed through it. "I see you're studying synaptic transmissions."

"The Academy won't let me test out of any subject."

"Why not?"

"Because I'm a female."

"I'm sorry, Sarah, I was not aware of their prejudiced attitudes. The Madrians medical facilities are some of the best, next to those on Khitan. Unfortunately, the Chirons don't take offworlders. I came to say goodbye. I didn't want to leave without seeing you again. I'm sorry we had so little time." When she didn't respond, he let his eyes linger a long moment on her. "Am I getting the silent treatment?" he asked.

"Oh no, please, don't think that. I just don't know what to say. I wish you didn't have to leave. But that sounds too much like I am feeling sorry for myself. I know there's no commitment on your part, and you never pretended more. Maybe I'm going to have your baby, and that should be enough for me."

"Sarah Love," he said, as he put his hand over hers, "I'm not walking away from you. You will always be a part in my life, and I wouldn't have it any other way."

Sarah looked up at him, but as always, his face was unreadable. She sighed and suddenly became aware of covert eyes watching them. "We are being scrutinized," she told him.

"Yes, I noticed. I can understand how intolerable this situation must be for you. If I were not on a mission, I would take you home right away. Only three more months, Sarah, and I will be back."

Chapter 4

Before leaving, Sargon stopped by the Embassy of Acheron. As a friend of Ambassador Aram Valdor ra Sandor he was immediately received. Sargon apprised him of Sarah and the situation which had developed because of her ignorance of Madras's cultural mores.

"Aram, I would like for you to talk to the President of the Academy. The dean might not be amenable, but some of her test papers have disappeared, and she is afraid she will fail or be dismissed. There is no reason for her to fail, I taught her myself."

"I will inform him of the harassment she has suffered and that her apartment had been ransacked. Will you come with me?"

"No, my alien looks might prejudice him toward Sarah."

"The Madrian's are xenophobic," Aram admitted. Then he suddenly smiled. "How is Sabrina?" he asked.

"She is well. She has graduated from the Space Academy and is now assigned to the Chiron starship Trefayne."

"Forgive my curiosity, but is Sarah anything like Sabrina?"

Sargon looked at him, then, started to laugh. "Sarah is a toned down version of Sabrina. She is gentler, but every bit as strong willed as her counterpart."

"Are you implying that I will have fewer problems with her?"

"Implying, but not promising. How is Thalia?"

"Right now, she is on Daugave. She will come by here and stay with me for a while before returning to Acheron. Don't worry about your charge, I will take care of her," Aram promised.

After Sargon left, Aram asked his secretary to set up an appointment with Ras al Khazim, the President of the Academy.

Chapter 5

Sarah was not too surprised when she received a notice to see the President of the Academy. She knew Sargon would not leave before helping with this situation as much as he could. When the day came, she dressed with care, and very conservatively.

The president's mansion was on campus grounds. As she walked up the stairs, the door was opened by a man-servant.

"I have an appointment with Ras al Khazim," she told him, and handed him her card.

His eyes flickered momentarily as he studied her dark face, then, said, "Will you please come in?"

Sarah was led immediately to Ras al Khazim's office. When the door opened, she was surprised to see Aram Valdor ra Sandor. "Mister Ambassador. How very kind of you to come."

"Captain Thalon would not have forgiven me," he told her, while his mien remained somber. "May I introduce you to Ras al Khazim?"

"Mr. President, thank you for receiving me." She glanced at him from under her long lashes. He was tall, and broad-shouldered. His hair was dark blond, his complexion fair, and his eyes a light brown. He was a handsome man.

Ras al Khazim looked at Sarah with undisguised astonishment. He had never seen anyone with such dark skin and was mesmerized by her large eyes. She didn't appear submissive, but exotic he decided, and became aware of his body's arousal.

"I was informed by my butler that it is almost lunch time. Would you like to join me?" he asked Aram.

"Sorry, Ras al Khazim, I have an appointment I can't miss. But thank you for your invitation."

"Miss Thalon?"

Sarah blushed, feeling put on the spot. Not being familiar with proprieties, she wasn't sure whether to accept or not. She hated to say no, so she agreed to stay. Sarah had grown up in the free society on the Antares where everyone was family, and she had yet to learn how to respond to subtleties.

"Miss Thalon," al Khazim smiled, warm and natural, "May I call you Sarah?"

"Please do."

"Since it is such a lovely day, I have arranged lunch to be served on the terrace."

Sarah spent the next hour exchanging polite inconsequentialities. He was the soul of tact, but when lunch was over, she was quite happy to escape.

* * *

It's been almost four years since I came here Sarah thought, as she leaned out the infirmary window, watching birds squabble in the yard. Suddenly, she was overwhelmed by a deep sense of loneliness. There was no real pain when she thought about Meshab. Sargon had taught her that if she kept her grievances inside, she was only hurting herself. So she let her anger and disgust go; to let it all flow under the bridge and down the river and out of sight. She smiled. It was a good metaphor to let disagreeable feelings dissipate. The air was still chilly around the hospital, but the persecutions stopped abruptly and she was grateful for that. She had written a letter of thanks to Aram Valdor ra Sandor and another to Ras al Khazim.

A sudden breeze ruffled her hair and she came out of her reverie. Two more months, she thought. Then she smiled. She was going home, and she was going to have Sargon's baby.

* * *

Today Sarah only had duty until early evening at the student's infirmary. Since the weather was still pleasant, she decided to walk home. As she passed the administration building, Ras al Khazim came walking toward her.

He stopped and smiled. "Sarah, how nice to see you again!" he said delighted.

Sarah blushed very slightly. "Good afternoon, Sir."

"Are you on your way to a class or something?"

"I just finished duty in the infirmary."

"Tedious job?"

"No, I like working with patients."

"There is going to be a faculty tea tomorrow on the university ground. Would you like to come as my guest?"

She was off tomorrow so agreed to come.

Sarah arrived at the time Ras al Khazim told her, but the tea was already in progress. If there had been a reception line, it had already dispersed. Al Khazim introduced her to Lisa Abrama, a woman she guessed to be somewhat younger than herself.

"You're doing your internship?" Lisa asked excitedly.

"Yes. I should be finished in another year."

"Aren't you excited about becoming a doctor?"

"Yes, very," Sarah said in a reserved tone.

Lisa pointed to Ras al Khazim, "Doesn't he look handsome and so very important? He comes from a very distinguished family."

"Is that so," Sarah replied noncommittally.

"Do you miss your family?" Lisa asked, artlessly.

"Yes, I do."

"Your parents?"

"They're dead," Sarah quickly injected.

"You have a guardian?"

"Yes. Captain Thalon." Sarah wondered why all these questions.

"al Khazim told me that you live on a worldship."

"Yes."

"Oh how interesting. Families live on this ship too?"

"Yes."

Lisa was becoming desperate, and she felt acutely uncomfortable. She was quite skillful in the social arts, but this was like pulling teeth to get Sarah Thalon to engage in a conversation. Sarah was either unsophisticated or a bore. "What do you do on a worldship?"

"Like the name says, it's a world, not very unlike a planet, except we live inside. I'm a physician when I'm home. I only came here to learn more about alien anatomy." Sarah stressed the word alien. "I also wanted to treat real cases. Antareans don't get sick very often. We don't have diseases on board." This was said with certain finality as Sarah turned toward Ras al Khazim who was coming toward them.

"I hope you enjoyed Lisa's company," he said encouragingly.

"I learned something about a worldship." Lisa interrupted, a little harassed. "And you know, she has a worldship captain as a guardian."

"Captain Thalon is your guardian?" He was not surprised. Recalling the same last name, he had already assumed that there might be a family relationship.

"Guardian is an approximate term Sarah explained. Family relationships on the Antares are complicated. Many of the terms are untranslatable," she lied. Sarah hated to be asked such personal questions. Also, being foisted on a strange female was not much to her liking. She wondered why he had invited her.

* * *

The following week, and to her utter irritation, Lisa Abrama came to visit her. When she saw Sarah's apartment, Lisa fastidiously wrinkled her nose. Sarah smiled. "I'm not here very often," she told her. "Most of my time is spent at the hospital."

"I know you work very hard, and I hope the results are rewarding, no?"

Sarah looked at her with a raised eyebrow.

"What do you usually do when you are off duty?" Lisa asked.

"I study. It shortens the time until I can go home."

"Are you not happy on Madras?"

Sarah evaded with, "I might be needed at home."

Lisa was not pleased. This was the most difficult assignment she had ever had. Working as an intermediary agent was not easy under the best of circumstances. Ras al Khazim expected her to gain Sarah's trust so she would divulge information about her family and lifestyle.

I bet he wants to know how much interference he would get, Lisa mused. Most Madrian women were well protected. They brought lucrative bride prices. He probably wants to know how much she knew of Madrian culture. Sarah's short answers left her with few openings to bring up other subjects.

Then, I don't know what he sees in her, she continued to muse. She is not even young anymore. I know he doesn't want Sarah as a wife because he has a wife who manages his town-house in Sikar and his finances. Maybe as a concubine? As far as I know he had already four. Maybe she was just a diversion, or temporary consort. If she was to become a temporary consort, Lisa speculated, he would have to draw up a contract to legitimate a child if they should have one. In all probability he would use her agency. Her agency had proven to be discrete before.

Sarah was still waiting impatiently to be told the reason for this visit. She knew it was not a social call, because she didn't move in the Madrian social sphere.

Lisa was still trying to decide if she should say she invited her, or al Khazim. She decided a straight approach would be better. "I was asked by Ras al Khazim to see if you're interested in going to a concert tonight."

"Why does he not ask me himself?"

She gave Sarah a shocked expression, thinking perhaps she has no sense of propriety. "It's not fitting for a gentleman to approach a woman. Especially when she is…single. This is usually done through an intermediary."

"Oh, I see. And is it proper for a single female to accept such invitations?"

Lisa smiled. "Not if she is accompanied by a chaperon."

"But I don't have a chaperon."

"I would gladly come with you. A very famous soloist is performing tonight. Say you will come. Otherwise, I can't either, because, I also need to be chaperoned."

For the first time Sarah laughed, thinking of Kamila. "You sound like a sister I have. Tell Ras al Khazim that I will come, but only so you can go to the concert."

Lisa gave a small smile that Sarah couldn't read.

"Now tell me, what does one wear to a concert?"

"I came early so we could go shopping. I know a nice little shop where you could find something appropriate."

* * *

Later that evening, Lisa arrived to collect Sarah close to the time the concert was supposed to start. To Sarah's surprise they went to a private home. She had expected the concert to be held in a theater; otherwise she would not have accepted the invitation.

When Sarah asked, Lisa patiently explained, "This is a special performance.

Our host, a very rich and powerful politician, engaged the soloist to perform for his private audience."

Arriving at the mansion, the two women entered a large hall covered with colorful tiles. The walls were alive with mosaics of flowers, trees, and brilliantly plumed birds, all lavishly painted. In the distance they could see male musicians playing on flutes and harps. al Khazim was standing close to the entrance, seemingly waiting for her. His eyes lightened when he saw Sarah in her magenta gown, her hair loose at her shoulders in a style Lisa promised would be very becoming.

Sarah wondered why she was not introduced to the host, or any of the other guests. When signaled by Ras al Khazim, Lisa guided Sarah toward two chairs placed just off the front row. Soon the other guests were moving toward their seats, giving Sarah and Lisa surreptitious looks. A sudden hush fell as the artist made his entrance. He was dark skinned with dark lascivious eyes and auburn hair. After he was seated, he began to stroke the harp with his long delicate fingers in a most sensuous manner, as if it were a woman. As he played, the strings evoked music that entranced all into harmony, peace and love. Sarah sat motionless.

Ras al Khazim was not only entranced by the music, but by Sarah's luminous eyes glistening with unshed tears, and the lovely smile that graced her lips.

When the last cord died away, Lisa touched Sarah's arm. "We need to leave. Ras al Khazim has many social responsibilities and should not be distracted from them. He has asked if you would like to go sailing tomorrow."

"Sailing? Oh yes." Sarah's face lit up. "Yes, I will." She remembered a planet under a beautiful sun and an endless ocean.

"I will pick you up. He said to be ready about nine o'clock in the morning."

Lisa arrived about seven the next morning with a parcel in her hands.

"Sarah, Ras al Khazim asked me to do some shopping for you since your work leaves you with little time." When she pulled back the wrapping, Sarah gave a gasp of surprise. The garments were made of fine silk. She held them up and gave Lisa an astonished look. "I thought we were going sailing?"

"These are the proper coverings for sailing. The sun will be hot and most women don't like their skin exposed."

Sarah shrugged. She had planed to wear a bikini and dive into the cool water and feel the freedom of moving with the wind. This was not going to be anything at all like she imagined. Disappointed, she dressed in the wide, loose slacks and overdress. Lastly, she put on the scarf to protect her hair.

When they arrived at the wharf, Ras al Khazim met them personally.

"Sarah, you look enchanting," he said. Then he complemented Lisa for choosing a very becoming color.

"Thank you. I'm content that it pleases you."

Sarah watched the two unobtrusively and wondered at the deference Lisa was showing toward Ras al Khazim.

On board, the two women sat in deck chairs away from the spray of water and wind. When Sarah tried to remove her scarf, Lisa quickly prevented her with, "Your hair will be blown all about."

Irritated, Sarah wanted to tell her tartly that her hair type did not blow easily about, but was forestalled by a steward bringing refreshments.

Ras al Khazim was steering the boat out to sea. Later on, stripped to his waist, he handled the sails, showing off his light tanned skin and rippling muscles. As he furled the sails, Lisa excused herself, complaining of a headache, and left to lie down below.

"Where's Lisa?" Ras al Khazim asked, as he came toward Sarah.

"She said she had a headache."

"Probably the sun's reflection on the water was too bright for her eyes."

"Then she should wear sunglasses," Sarah quipped

"It would spoil her beauty."

Sarah gave him an amused look.

"I've had very little time to talk with you. I hope you enjoyed Lisa's company. Have you been sailing before?"

"Yes, many times."

"Your studies coming along well?"

"Yes."

"You have only one more year until you receive your diploma?"

"I'm leaving in two months. Captain Thalon is coming back to take me home."

There was tightness in his chest as he stared ahead. He looked at her, and pondered. She was not so young, not like his Lyra, who was just fifteen. But she was still beautiful and exotic. And he desired her as he had not desired a woman in a long time. His plan had been to move cautiously and win her trust. But now?

"Oh, but that is too soon. I had hoped to show you some of the beauty of Madras. Why don't we go to the botanical garden tomorrow? You can't leave before seeing the flowers in full bloom."

"Tomorrow I'm on duty."

"Then next day?"

"Perhaps for a while, in the afternoon. I do have to study."

Raz sighed. "Then I will have to be content with that."

* * *

Ras al Khazim planned a whirlwind of activities for her. They went to the botanical garden several times. It was so huge and could not be savored in one day. He showed her the most famous waterfalls on Madras, and they went to the theater together. Most of the time, they were alone. It was a relief when Lisa was nowhere to be seen. Sarah enjoyed his company. Despite her earlier reluctance, she began to admire him, noticing his elegance and comportment. When Raz looked at her, his glance was inscrutable and she wondered what he was thinking. His manners were always correct, and he never touched her.

Raz was impressed by her intelligence and openness. Sarah did not sport the wiles he was accustomed to from the women, nor their fawning. On one moonlit night, while sitting on the beach, he asked her to marry him.

Sarah was taken aback. "But I can't," she told him.

"Why not, Sarah?"

"I'm pregnant."

She was conscious of his silence.

"What will you do with the child?" he finally asked.

She looked at him in surprise. "I will raise it."

Ras al Khazim sat thinking, trying not to look at her. He was wise in the ways of women and recognized Sarah as unique. When she spoke, her voice was firm and resonant, not like the whispering voices of his other women. When they spoke, they meekly bent their heads and let their lashes fall. Sarah looked straight at him and he marveled at her black eyes. When their color deepened, they became like limpid pools to drown in. The need to posses this exquisite beauty was consuming him.

He had planned his strategies carefully, knowing he must first win her trust, and not to alarm her, either by gesture or touch. He was even more determined to possess her. But the child was an unexpected inconvenience. He quickly considered an alternative possibility. Maybe an old aunt would like to raise a baby. There was a widowed sister of his mother who never had a child. She might like to take it. Suddenly, he roused himself out of his reveries and bent down to touch her lightly on the shoulder. She lifted her head and regarded him in silence. "It doesn't matter, Sarah. The child will be welcome."

That was not what she had expected. After a thoughtful silence she said, "Ras al Khazim, I will consider it. But for now, I'd like to go back to my apartment."

Chapter 6

Sarah lay in bed thinking. Thinking about what to do. She knew she should go home. But she had enjoyed her time with Ras al Khazim, so correct, so gentle and considerate. Agitated, she rose and began to pace. If I just stay one more year she reasoned, I will have my diploma. Then she thought of home. She would only be alone. Everyone was gone. The Antares was empty of people. Where could she go? Being around Sargon, she was conscious of restlessness and longing for something she did not know what. When she thought of Sargon, all the feelings were there. She still wanted him, and with a wry smile she admitted just as much as Sabrina. Making love to him had awakened all the old yearnings.

Now there was Ras al Khazim's promise. Sargon had made none. Staying here would mean the end of her loneliness. She would have companionship, maybe even love and a home. Before dawn, she finally fell asleep. When she awakened, even before opening her eyes, she knew she would accept Ras al Khazim's proposal.

Sarah sent a communiqué to Sargon explaining her intent to stay on Madras. She told him that Ras al Khazim's proposed, despite her being pregnant, and that she had accepted his offer of marriage.

* * *

A month later, there was a simple ceremony and they both signed a contract. After the signing, he took her hands into his and gazed deeply into her eyes, then without a pang of conscience, lied. He explained that after a year's time, if they were still together, the family would hold an elaborate ceremony and she would be accepted into his family. For now, it would only be the two of them. When she asked why she couldn't meet his family now, he was evasive. He only reiterated that only after a year's time, if they were still together, would he be allowed to present her to his family.

Ras rented an apartment in Port City. When all was in readiness, he brought his bride home. The apartment was a suite that covered the second story of a house. When she asked why they were not living in the mansion, he explained that it belonged to the university, and that he only had an apartment there and the rooms to entertain in. It wouldn't be proper for him to live there with his wife. Also, all the furniture had been selected by him before they moved in. But she didn't mind at all being taken care of. For the first time in her life, she was happy. He was kind; he was gentle, and an ardent and experienced lover. He didn't interfere with her work, since he was often required to stay late at the office himself.

One day as she returned home, the door was opened by an elderly woman with a sour expression on her face.

"Good afternoon," Sarah said politely, as she entered her hallway.

The woman bowed slightly. "Good afternoon. I'm Asur. I used to be Ras' amah. He has asked me to serve him once again," she enlightened Sarah.

"Welcome to my home. I'm delighted to meet you," Sarah greeted her, genuinely pleased.

★ ★ ★

Sarah thought she would enjoy Azur's company, and would welcome help doing the housework. As it turned out, Azur was a sloven. The apartment always looked untidy and Sarah had to do most of the cleaning herself. Azur was also an indifferent cook. Since Ras al Khazim was frequently absent, explaining that he had too much work, Sarah developed the habit of taking long walks before going home. Often her steps led her past the administration building where his office was located. The windows would be dark and the building closed up. When she asked, he reminded her of his social obligations. She also asked why she wasn't invited to any of his social functions.

"But Sarah, don't you think it would be too strenuous to stand around in your condition?" he soothed, patting her cheek. She loved his concern for her, but slowly began to wonder where he was when he stayed away from home.

One day he brought her a present. She opened it to find it contained a ledger. Surprised, she asked what he expected her to do with it.

"Sarah, you have a household now, and a household has expenses. You need to be more responsible and keep track of the money," he said in an instructive voice like she was an imbecile. It was the first time she was really annoyed with him. The money he was so concerned about was all hers in the first place. It came from the account Sargon had set up for her before she came to Madras. The income was also supplemented by her earnings as an intern. Ras had given her a little money here and there, but never enough for him to claim that he was paying for the household expenses.

Soon, he began to do all the household shopping and bill paying. Before long, she realized that he had taken control of her money. In the beginning, she was busy with her internship, and was glad he took care of things. Only too late did she realize what he was doing. He was making her dependent on him for everything.

* * *

Sarah was in her eighth month of pregnancy, when she received a call to come to Space Port Central. "We set up a visual with Captain Thalon from the Antarean Starship Explorer," the technician told her. When Sargon came on screen, he scrutinized her closely. What he saw was a happy face.

"Do I pass inspection?" she teased him.

"You look well."

"I feel fat."

"I have a favor to ask."

"I thought you called because you missed me."

"That too. Could you take care of Elisheba for me? She is very unhappy with me right now and I thought it would be good for the two of you to be together. She has gone through some harrowing times, and I know you will be patient with her. Since I don't think she will tell you all of the truth, I will send you her record. As a sister and physician I know you will be able to help her. "

"Do I have time to consult with my husband?"

"Yes. I will call back in twenty minutes."

For the first time since living together, Sarah called Ras al Khazim at his office.

Raz was puzzled when the secretary told him his wife was on the phone. He nearly dropped the receiver when he recognized Sarah's voice.

"Ras, Captain Thalon just called and asked if it would be convenient for my sister Elisheba to come and stay with us for a while."

There was a long silence as Ras al Khazim chewed on his thumb, thinking rapidly. "How long would she be with us?"

"I don't know."

He thought it might make things easier if Sarah had some diversions since he needed to spend some time at home with his wife in Sikar. He also needed to check on his concubines at his mountain estate, so he would be gone for a lengthy time. "I think we could manage it," he told her with a reassuring voice. "It would be good for you to have family around just now. Tell Captain Thalon that she would be welcome to stay with us as long as she desires."

When Sarah turned away from the screen, the technician handed her several sheets of paper just off the printer. The writing was in English, telling her of Sabrina's ill-fated expedition and Elisheba's tragedy. She was just finished reading and thinking about how to handle this situation with Elisheba, when the technician touched her shoulder. "Miss Thalon, the Captain of the Explorer is back on screen."

She looked at the background. "Sargon, where is Elisheba?"

"Waiting in the transporter room. Then it is a go?"

"Yes. She can stay with us as long as she wants to."

"Good, I'm sending her down. Take care of yourself." He smiled as he signed off.

Five minutes later, Elisheba walked through the door. "Elisheba Love, how are you? I'm so glad to see you," Sarah exclaimed with outstretched arms, enfolding her in a tight embrace.

"Hello Sarah," Elisheba said. "It's good to see you again. Then paused, "You're pregnant!"

"No kidding. Sargon's baby."

"But Sargon said you are married?"

"It happened before I met Ras, and he is accepting the baby. Ras is very nice, you'll like him."

"You look happy enough."

"I am, very. Where do we pick up your luggage?"

"It's just outside the door."

Leaning against the wall was a duffle bag.

"A duffle bag? That's all?" was Sarah's quizzical response.

"Easiest traveling kit." As they walked toward the exit, Elisheba asked, "Do you know where any of the others are?"

"I only know that Sabrina was on Acheron, but is now on the starship Trefayne. Ayhlean's on Sigma IV, and Kamila on Ganymede."

"You hear from them?"

"I had a letter from Ayhlean not to long ago," Sarah told her, waving for a taxi.

"She's okay?"

"As far as I know."

Elisheba stared at the taxi and asked, "You remember the old movies we used to watch?"

"You mean the ones we had about Earth?"

"Yes." She grunted as she hoisted her duffle bag into the trunk. "And don't you think this looks somewhat like it?"

"Technologically, the Madrians are where we were in the fifties. I'm not too familiar with their culture though. I've rarely been outside Port City, except once to work in a children's hospital, and another time to look at a famous waterfall. As an intern, I don't have much free time, but I hope this will change. I got my diploma a month ago, but I still work reduced hours at the hospital. So, maybe we could go on a trip into Shikar. It's supposed to be a big city. Maybe Ras will show us around."

When they arrived at the apartment house, Ras was waiting for them downstairs.

"My husband," Sarah introduced him proudly in Galactic. "Ras, this is my sister Elisheba."

"Welcome to Madras, Elisheba," he said politely, looking astonished at her red hair and thinking what a handsome wench. Elisheba was tall and willowy with a light, delicate complexion. If they are sisters, I'm not my mother's son he thought, but only said, "You travel lightly," and relieved the, at this time, more attentive driver of the duffle bag. When Elisheba only inclined her head, he told Sarah, "Asur has prepared a room for our guest." Sarah looked at Ras and refrained to remark. Asur was not very conscientious about her household duties. Actually, she was very indolent, making a big show around Ras. One day, after coming home, she found Asur sitting in the kitchen having kava with the woman she had hired to help Asur to clean the house. She had left the kitchen trying to decide how to confront her. She thought of Kamila and tried to picture how she would handle such a situation. After the cleaning woman left, Sarah had gone to Asur's room. Leaning against the door-frame in the same manner she knew Kamila would do and mimicking her insolent voice, she asked Azur, "Do you regale all your help in this manner? They don't come here to work, only to drink your kava and waste Ras's money." It had worked.

When Sarah opened the door to the guest room, she saw the hastily thrown together bed. Dust lay on the floor and furniture. She gave Elisheba an apologetic look. "We'll clean this after he leaves," she told her in English.

Ras gave Azur a peremptory order to bring refreshment, then, led Elisheba toward the living room.

Elisheba was about as informative as Sarah had been when it came to discussing the family structure and culture on the Antares. Naturally, he was very curious and wanted to know how she and Sarah were related.

Sarah chuckled. Looking from Ras to Elisheba she said, "I told him that family connections on the Antares are complicated and many terms are untranslatable."

"That's about the gist of it," Elisheba agreed.

* * *

When Sarah arrived at work the next morning, she found the surgical ward filled with patients. As she passed an orderly, he stopped her and looked at his clipboard, "You're supposed to assist the chief surgeon this morning. You better hurry."

"Where is his assistant?"

"He called in sick."

Sarah entered the operating room. "You better scrub," the physician

39

told her. "You wanted a wide range of experience. You're going to get it. The patient has a subdural aneurism."

When she came home late that night, her legs were tired from standing, and her back ached. Her brain shut down a long time ago, and she ran on automatic responses. As she passed one of the guest rooms, she heard a muffled cry, and a resounding slap on flesh. Had she not been so tired she would have investigated. She only stopped at Elisheba's room and peeked in. Elisheba was sound asleep.

Early next morning Sarah was again in a hurry and went to the kitchen to grab a quick breakfast. Azur was in the kitchen pretending to work. Also, a girl no more than twelve or thirteen, sat huddled in a corner.

"Who is this?" she asked Azur.

"Oh, this is only a niece of mine. Say hello to the lady," Azur told her.

There was a shy and barely audible, "Good morning, Lady Sabrina," in Galactic.

"She speaks Galactic?"

"Yes, and she is staying with us for a while."

"That's okay I guess. Does Ras know? Sorry I have to go." She quickly wrote a note for Elisheba, then, grabbed a piece of bread and an apple to eat on the run.

For the next several days she was constantly needed at the hospital, leaving early and returning home late. She felt guilty because there had been so little time to spend with Elisheba. Both had agreed to rise earlier in the morning to at least have a few moments together. Sarah had yet to have an opportunity to touch on the expedition. Also, it didn't take her long to notice that she did most of the talking. Elisheba appeared too somber. The happy, bubbly girl she remembered seemed to have vanished.

Finally the pace slackened, and to make amends, Sarah went to the market to buy the ingredients to make spaghetti, Elisheba favorite, and a bunch of flowers. When she opened the door to the apartment, Ras met her in the hall. She was greeted with, "Your sister has left. She said she was going home."

Sarah stared at him in stunned silence as the grocery bag slipped unheeded to the floor. She groped for support and leaned against the wall. "She did what?" Sarah asked, incredulous. "Ras that is something Elisheba would never do. What happened?"

"What happened," he snapped. "How should I know? She tore out of here saying something about catching a ship."

"Ras, you don't just catch a ship. What ship? This behavior is extraordinary, and very unlike Elisheba."

"Well, she might not have liked staying here all by herself. Maybe she was bored. Have you ever thought about that?"

In a flare of anger, Sarah minced her words slowly and deliberate. "She wasn't bored. She cleaned the filthy kitchen, she scoured the filthy bathrooms. She was so busy she didn't have time to be bored." The appearance of the apartment had been a contention between them ever since Azur had moved in. Sarah couldn't abide the filth and often cleaned it herself after she'd come home tired from work.

"There is no reasoning with women," Ras said, exasperated.

When Sarah reached for her overcoat, Ras grabbed her arm, "You are not leaving this house without my permission."

Sarah yanked her arm free and ran out of the house and hailed a taxi. "Space Central," she told the driver. Leaning back into the seat she racked her brain to explain Elisheba's behavior. Something extraordinary must have happened for her to leave like that, especially without a word to her. When the taxi arrived at Space Central, Sarah paid the driver and hurried toward the building. To her ears, her footsteps sounded overly loud on the pavement as she ran up the white granite stairs and through the two double glass doors.

The Ensign on duty tried to stop her. "No civilians are allowed in here," he told her.

"I am Commander Sarah Thalon of the Worldship Antares. I need to see the logs of all outgoing ships."

He stood at attention, but looked a little flustered at her.

Sarah looked at him and then followed to where his eyes were resting. "What's your name Ensign?"

"Tebor, Ma'am."

"Ensign Tebor, even Commanders get pregnant," she told the blushing youth. "Now, how about helping me a little? Where do I find the rosters of outgoing ships?"

"Lieutenant Tejur could help you."

"Well Ensign, show me the way."

He led her out of the building and across the plaza to the tower. Exiting the lift, Ensign Tebor approached the office of Lieutenant Tejur. The Ensign was standing at attention and blushing to the roots of his hair again. "Lieutenant, Sir, Commander Sarah Thalon from the Worldship Antares would like to see you, Sir."

Lieutenant Tejur turned out to be a young Madrian. As Sarah approached, he raised his eyes reluctantly. Another damned female, he thought. He hated when they pulled rank on him. "Can I see some identification?" he asked, disdainfully.

Sarah handed him her ID.

He checked it carefully, then handed it back. "What is it that I can do for you?"

"I need to contact Dock Central and see the roster of all outgoing ships."

"I don't know…"

Lieutenant, I am a Commander, and you will stand at attention."

The Lieutenant rose with more animation than he had shown until now, and the Ensign had a hard time hiding his grin.

"You will contact Dock Central, and you will show me the display of all out going ships." The display showed only one ship, a merchant vessel, to have left Dock Central. "Patch me though to personnel," Sarah demanded.

At personnel, a sleepy voiced Ensign answered.

"Ensign, this is Commander Thalon. I want the roster of the Merchant Vessel Doran."

When the Ensign hesitated, Lieutenant Tejur snapped. "Ensign, I want the roster showing on my monitor, now."

Sure enough, Elisheba's name was on the roster. "Thank you Lieutenant. Now, I need a message patched through to the Antares, the Explorer, and Daugave."

"Daugave?" Tejur asked.

"Yes. I need to reach an Alliance member who might be there. Lieutenant, I wouldn't do this if it weren't necessary. So please cooperate. Now, put me through to communications."

When communications came on and Tejur informed them

of his request, the answer was, "We don't allow civilians to send communications through starship channels."

Sarah took a deep breath. She looked closer at the uniform. "You're a W-2, right?"

"Yes, Ma'am."

"You see, I'm a Commander. I'm in civilian clothes because this is an emergency. The message, I am sending is a distress call; and I want it to show on my screen also. Now send," and she spelled out the English message, Captain Thalon. Emergency. Elisheba fled Madras. She is on the merchant vessel Doran. Sarah. Send this to the Antares, the Explorer, and to Daugave right now."

She waited until the message was sent, then turned to leave. All the way home, she racked her brain. What had happened? What could have made Elisheba leave? Did Ras say something to her? No. It must have been something terribly serious.

Sarah had barely stepped through the door of her apartment when Ras grabbed her arm and flung her around to face him. "You will never again leave this place without my permission," he hissed, his face livid. Turning to Azur who suddenly appeared, "She is not to leave the house by herself again. You will accompany her wherever she goes." Rounding on Sarah, "I will call the hospital and tell them that you are not feeling well. Now give me your keys, you won't need them anymore."

Sarah handed him the keys, knowing this was not the time to pursue an argument. She ignored Azur's gloating and retired to her room to lie down. She was awake nearly half the night, trying to figure out what could have happened, and Ras's unreasonable behavior. He had changed over the months. At first, it was imperceptible. Then there were the unexplained absences. Money had become an issue. There never seemed to be enough money, even though she used her own to pay for household expenses. Lately, he had become irritated about her pregnancy. She was getting too big for him to enjoy his nighttime activities. Now she felt foolish for passing up the chance to go home. But the first five or six months of her marriage had been happy ones.

* * *

The next morning Azur left and locked Sarah in. After examining the lock, Sarah smiled. Picking it would be no problem. She was certain

Ras had made good on his threat to call the hospital to give a plausible explanation for her absence. She spent the morning going through her closet and drawers, sorting her things. She packed what she needed into her duffle bag. When she came to the jewelry he had given her, she considered each item, then shrugged and put them back. She didn't care to take any. Then she went into the nursery. She looked at the crib, dresser, and baby furniture she had purchased. It didn't matter. As soon as the baby was born, she would take passage to go home. She knew Ras' domineering behavior would only escalate, and that was no environment she wanted her child to grow up in.

By mid-afternoon, she fixed herself something to eat, then picked the lock and went for a walk. When she returned later in the evening, Azur met her in the hallway.

"How did you get out?" she asked, incensed.

"Through the door," Sarah pointed.

"If you don't behave, you'll get into trouble. I will tell Ras al Khazim."

"Get out of my way. Don't cross my path again," she told Azur in a very quiet voice. She left Azur standing open mouthed in the hall, and going into the kitchen, she again fixed herself something to eat.

Later that night, she was awakened by a muffled cry. She sat up to listen, thinking she must have been dreaming. Then she heard it again and stepped into the hallway. Again, there was a resounding slap. Immediately, Sarah knew where it came from. She opened the door and turned on the light. She gave a gasp when she saw Ras on his back in the bed, and the girl she'd seen in the kitchen, straddled on top of him.

"You… you…" she had no words for him.

Ras flung the girl off and launched himself at Sarah. She quickly sidestepped, and using his body's velocity, slammed his head into the wall. The wall shook as he bounced off. When he looked at her, he was more astonished than mad. He turned slowly, and came at her with his open hand. She slapped it away, then, Karate punched him in the face. When he came at her again, she grabbed him by his collar and pushed his face into he wall.

"I want you out of this apartment. I want the keys on my kitchen table, and you can take your lazy slut of an amah with you." She gave him one more push toward the door.

Ras left, slamming the door behind him.

A whimper made Sarah turn around. The girl stood on the bed with one leg crossed over the other, and her hand pressed against the lower part of her abdomen. There was a trickle of blood running down her legs.

"Oh my God!" Sarah exclaimed. "Come, let's go to my bedroom." The girl was stiff and frightened as Sarah picked her up and carried her to her bedroom. Putting her down on her bed she asked, "What's your name?"

"Nala."

"Is Azur your aunt?"

"No."

A terrible thought started to grow in Sarah's mind. Why would a man abuse a child? What kind of man would abuse a child? Where did this child come from? Sarah went to the bathroom to get a wet washrag. When she came back to the bed, she said "Nala, I need to clean you up and look to see where you are injured. I'm not trying to hurt you, but I have to see." She gently spread the girl's legs and cleaned the semen and blood away. Then she probed, hoping she was gentle enough. The girl was torn and in need of surgery. Suddenly a tearing pain made her gasp and double over. With effort she straightened up and her hand went to her back. Oh my God she thought I'm going into labor.

Sarah waited until the pain subsided, then went to the phone to call the hospital for star fleet personnel. When the phone was answered she said, "This is Commander Sarah Thalon of the Worldship Antares. I'm going into premature labor, and I also have a ward who has been raped."

"You want us to send an ambulance?"

"Yes please," she said, then, grunted with another contraction.

The hospital for the alliance fleet personnel was mostly staffed by offworlders who toke care of aliens needing medical attention. After she informed Sargon that she would stay on Madras, he advised her to choose this facility, instead of having Madrian personnel take care of her. Before the ambulance came, Sarah had several more spasms and Nala looked worried. Sarah told her, "The baby is coming."

At the hospital Sarah expected to fill out an admission record and was surprised to learn that one already existed.

"We have all the information about you. The only thing we need is to make out a birth-certificate for the baby. For this, we need the father's name and position."

"The father's name is…" Sarah looked momentarily confused at the nurse, who in turn gave her a curious look.

"Give me the record," Sarah told her peremptorily. Her eyes quickly scanned the information. It recorded her age, height, skin color and rank. Down at the very bottom was a signature. She recognized Sargon's handwriting. It was signed Captain J. Thalon.

"Oh my, my, my," Sarah said in her best Sabrina imitation. "I'm glad he put his name on it." Turning to the nurse, "All right then, put Jim Thalon as the father's name." When Sarah looked at the nurse she noticed an amused and knowing smile on her face. "Have you ever seen Captain Thalon?"

"Yes. I was there when he filled out your medical and personnel record."

"Good. When my baby is born, come and look at its eyes. I don't think you will have any doubt that it is Captain Thalon's child."

The amused smile disappeared and she said, "But we need to make one for the girl."

"Nala," Sarah said, "tell the nurse your name."

"Nala," the girl answered.

"Your other name?"

"I don't have another name."

Just then, one of the doctors came in. "She probably doesn't remember her family name," he said as he looked at Nala.

"Explain," Sarah demanded.

"Sometimes poor parents sell their daughters into service."

Sarah looked at him, perplexed. "And men buy them?"

"Sometimes the wives to gain relief from their husband's inopportune sexual demands."

"But a small child?"

"Sometimes they are even younger."

"That's monstrous," Sarah said, and thought of Ras al Khazim. He had been so gentle with her, although demanding at times. Then she remembered when his attention became painful, he would go away and sulk.

"What name are we going to put on Nala's record?" the nurse wanted to know.

"Nala Thalon."

"No parents?"

"No, ward of Commander Sarah Thalon."

"Thalon? I'm sorry, I didn't introduce myself. I'm doctor Tersus. I have a friend named Captain Thalon."

"Same Thalon," Sarah quipped, and bit down on her lip to endure another contraction.

Doctor Tersus smiled. "I will take care of Nala and call the embassy of Acheron to legitimate your ward. Doctor Ren will take care of you. She's a Chiron and skillful in alien anatomy"

Chapter 7

Sarah's daughter, born eight hours later, was of normal size and weight.

Her skin was slightly lighter then Sarah's and she had light brown eyes with golden flecks in them. Her pupils became yellow slits as they contracted in the glaring light. When Sarah tried to bond with her, her attempts were rejected.

Startled, Sarah looked up at Drs. Ren.

"You tried to bond?" she asked.

"Yes. But she ..." and then Sarah looked puzzled, "she closed down."

"Commander Thalon..."

"Sarah, please."

"Sarah, being born is a strenuous journey for a small one. Many babies reject the intrusion at first. Give her some rest and then try again." Then after a moments thought, "You never did that before?"

"No. Captain Thalon said to bond with her right away was very important."

"Yes. I understand. Since the birth was without complication and the infant is normal size, you can be transferred to your room now."

"Thank you Doctor Ren."

As Sarah was wheeled toward her room holding the baby in her arms, she noticed that she had acquired a shadow. Nala was following close behind the gurney.

"What are you doing here? Shouldn't you be in bed?"

The girl cringed and her eyes silently pleaded as she looked up at

Sarah. "Please Sarah, let me stay with you. Don't let them take me away."

Sarah could see Nala's distress and asked the nurse, "Could you put a cot in my room?"

"Yes of course. We tried to make her stay in her room, but she wouldn't. She shouldn't be walking around either, just coming out of surgery."

Later, when Sarah nursed her baby, she tried again to bond. This time she was accepted. The baby also accepted her name, Davida.

When Doctor Tersus came in, Nala dived under her blankets. Sarah looked quizzically at Tersus. "Why is she frightened of you?"

"Because I questioned her."

"Why?"

"To understand your situation so I can advise you. Nala said that you are Ras al Khazim's temporary consort."

"I'm his wife," Sarah protested.

"No Lady, that's impossible."

"Why?"

"On Madras, a man can only have one wife, but many concubines. Sometimes men have temporary consorts. Did you and he sign a contract?"

"Yes. As I understood, it was a marriage contract."

"He lied to you."

"He must have done that a lot."

"Commander…Sarah, Ras al Khazim comes from an illustrious family. Very prominent, and very rich. His wife Renara takes care of their finances, and she is a very intelligent lady. Ras also has four concubines who manage an estate outside of Sikar.

"Boy, he sounds like a busy beaver," Sarah mumbled to herself in English.

"Pardon?" Tersus asked.

Sarah only gave him a woeful smile.

There was a hint of a reciprocal smile on Tersus's lips when he continued. "According to Madrian law, when you signed this document, you became Ras al Khazim's property…"

"I did what?" Sarah looked at him, stunned.

"He never explained Madrian law to you?"

"No, nor its customs. In hindsight, he was very reticent when I asked. When I asked about his family, he said something about having to be married for a year before he was allowed to present me to them."

"That's nonsense, but it was the best he could probably come up with. You also need to know that everything you own, belongs to him. He can restore it, if he so chooses. Any child born to you belongs to him," Tersus said, pointing to Davida."

Davida, now sated and securely bonded to her mother, was sound asleep. Sarah handed him the child. "Wake her and look at her eyes," Sarah told him.

Tersus took Davida into his arms and gently pocked her cheeks. Annoyed, she opened her eyes and the bright light made her pupils contract. "Captain Thalon's eyes?" Tersus said, surprised.

"Yes," Sarah said, and smiled proudly.

* * *

After being discharged from the hospital, Sarah, accompanied by her constant shadow, Nala, went to the communication Center at Space Port Central. It was her luck that Lieutenant Tejur was coming down the hallway toward them.

"Lieutenant Tejur, I think fate has sent you to help me again," she greeted the young man.

He was initially nonplussed at being addressed so informally by a woman wearing a loose and long flowing dress, until he looked at her more closely, then, grinned. "Ahhh, Commander Sarah Thalon," he said, remembering her.

Gesturing at Davida sleeping in the hammock-sling draped over her shoulder, and nudging Nala out from behind her, she said, "We would like to contact the Antarean Starship Explorer."

Tejur didn't spare a look at Nala, and gave the content of the sling only a cursory look when he said, "If you will come with me, I'll see if that's possible."

Sarah followed him as he walked back the way he had come, and then rode a lift up to the Control Tower. Again, she was greeted with, "Civilian's are not all…"

Sarah held up her hand, "I know. I'm Commander Sarah Thalon

and I need to contact the Antarean Starship Explorer. Would you send this code?" She gave a slip of paper to the controller.

"It may take time," she was told.

"I understand. Lieutenant Tejur, you may return to duty. Thank you for your assistance."

"Commander." He saluted before he left.

Sarah finally acknowledged the tuck on her dress. "What is it, Nala?"

Nala looked frightened and pointed to all the screens and monitors.

"You have never been in a room like this before?"

"No, Sarah. What are they going to do to us?" Nala whispered, apprehensively.

Sarah stared at her, at first not comprehending. Then she took Nala's chin in her hand and lifted her head. "Sweety, it's all right. There's nothing here to be afraid of. Those are just machines." Looking at the controllers sleeve and his name tag, then asked, "Lieutenant Marash, could you scrounge up a hand held communicator for me? I shall have it returned when it's not needed."

His face still registered reluctance, but he replied with a sharp, "Yes, Ma'am," and turned to the Sergeant in the room, ordering him to procure the needed equipment.

While they waited, Sarah played with Davida, then, nursed her, the sling effectively obscuring the activity. Davida just burped when the Sergeant handed her the communicator. Everyone became cognizant of what had been going on.

After three hours, communication from the Explorer finally came in. "Put it on screen," Sarah commanded. When the static cleared, the bridge came into focus. In the foreground was a stranger.

"This is the Explorer. Captain Suzago Murasaki. We received a priority call."

"This is the Madrian control tower. A Commander Sarah Thalon has requested the contact with the Antarean Starship Explorer."

"Commander Thalon, what's your priority?" Murasaki asked.

"I was given this coded message by Captain Thalon."

"Captain, Sir," she heard Yoshi speaking in the background. "May I, please?"

Yoshi came on screen, "Sarah!" he exclaimed. "I thought I recognized your voice."

"Yoshi." then in English, "I need a pick up."

"Are you in trouble?"

"Sort of. When can you pick me up?"

"E.T.A..." Sarah saw him turn around. "When can we make Madras, Benjie?"

"In about six hours. Say hi for me," he told Yoshi.

"Benjie says hi. But I guess you heard." Joshi laughed.

"I have a hand-communicator. I want you to key into it. I might need to be rescued. There are three of us to be beamed up."

Suddenly Benjie's face was on screen. "Did you multiply?" he asked, amused.

"Yes, sort of. Meet my daughter, Davida," and she held the baby up for them to see. Pushing Nala to the forefront, "and this is my ward, Nala Thalon."

"Okay, activate your communicator and let's key it in," Yoshi said. It only took seconds for it to be accomplished.

"I will keep it open. Close to your arrival time, I will go back to my apartment to pick up some of my things there. So, don't lose me."

"Okay. See you later."

Sarah breathed a sigh of relief. Six hours didn't seem too long. After the Explorer signed off, she thanked Marash. Repositioning Davida in her sling, then, herding Nala in front of her, she left.

* * *

Sarah took Nala to a small restaurant in Port City where she also had to nurse Davida, who had been exceptionally quiet. Afterwards, they went to the Embassy of Acheron. At the reception desk, Sarah gave her name, and requested to see the Ambassador. The receptionist only looked at her briefly before she rose. There was a standing order for Sarah to be admitted without delay.

Aram Valdor ra Sandor rose from his chair as soon as she came though the door. "Lady Sarah, please come in." He ushered her into his office, then looked surprised at Nala. She was without a doubt from Madras.

When he gave Sarah a questioning look, she said, "May I introduce my ward, Nala Thalon."

"I see. Is she registered under that name?" he asked.

"She has a medical record under that name, and Doctor Tersus told me that he informed your embassy about Nala's status."

"That should do it. What can I do for you?"

"Something I should have done a long time ago. I should have visited your embassy before. But I never dreamed that I would need help. Has Captain Thalon informed you that I married a Madrian named Ras al Khazim?

"Yes. And he asked us to help you if the need should arise."

"It has arisen," Sarah told him with a depreciating smile. "I was made to understand that I am only a temporary consort, and not wife to Ras al Khazim. I was always under the impression that we were married. There is a contract which is binding on me, but not Ras al Khazim. I need to know how to get this contract nullified. Can you give me a book, or booklets, to familiarize myself with the prevailing laws and customs of Madras?"

"You don't...I thought Thalon would have informed you before you came here."

"I guess he was remiss in that. I sent an emergency signal to the Antarean Starship Explorer and they are en route to pick me up..." looking at her watch, "in about five hours."

"Are you in trouble?"

"Ras el Khazim and I had a horrible falling out. He might get mean. The last time I saw him, he had a bloody nose," she told. Then she related Nala's story.

Aram Valdor gave her an appraising look. "You and the children could stay here. I have a small sitting room near my office. If you need anything, just tell my secretary."

"You are very kind. I am grateful. It would help if we could stay hidden."

Aram Valdor ra Sandor gave her several booklets containing excerpts of Madras' laws and customs. He offered a coloring book to Nala.

* * *

After three hours of having to be still, Nala became restless. Sarah looked at her watch. Still two more hours, she thought. Turning to Nala, "Would you like to go for a walk?"

Nala's face brightened, but immediately clouded over. "What are we going to do if he sees us?" she asked, bleakly

"We'll be careful. We need to find out where Ras is going to be. There are still things I need from the apartment. What is his wife's name again?"

"Renara."

"Okay. I will pretend that I'm Renara calling to check if he's still in the office. You think that will work?"

Nala looked doubtful. "The secretary will know you're not her."

"She knows Renara's voice?"

"I think so. But I could call and say that Lady Renara al Khazim would like to know if her husband is on his way home." Nala suddenly broke into a broad grin. "I could mimic Azur's voice."

"Okay, we might try that. But for now, we'll walk by the Administration building and see what we can see. Then we'll go and watch the apartment for a while before going in."

They arrived on campus without incident. Nala, still wary, scrutinized everyone who passed, keeping a watchful eye on their surroundings.

"Nala Love, we're going to be all right," Sarah assured her, and patted her on the shoulder.

"I'm still scared. Maybe someone will see us and tell him." She looked up at Sarah, "I don't have to go back to him, or to Azur?"

"No Nala, you're coming with me."

The girl's face relaxed and she gave Sarah a tiny shy smile.

They entered the Student Union, which was right across the administration building and went up to the second floor. They settled down at a window overlooking the parking lot.

"His car isn't there," Nala said.

"That doesn't mean much."

"I know."

There was quite a bit of activity, but they never saw anyone from his office. After an hour passed, Sarah asked Nala to make her phone call. Nala dialed his office. When the phone was answered, she mimicked

Azur's voice to perfection and said "This is Azur, my lady would like to know if Ras al Khazim has left his office to go home for the day?"

"Yes. He left quite some time ago."

"Thank you," Nala said and quickly hung up. "He's left for home already," she told Sarah.

"Now, we go to the apartment and watch it for a while."

Sarah and Nala stationed themselves up one floor. When she told Nala to sit on the steppes, she asked, "What are we going to do if someone asks what we're doing here?"

"I don't think anybody will come up the stairs. Most people ride the elevator. So, we'll just sit here and watch from the window." After about twenty minutes later Sarah saw Azur exit the bus and come waddling up the street.

"Nala, I think we let the cat out of the bag when we called his office. Azur's coming. Let's move up one more floor."

The elevator doors opened and Azur, with the keys in her hand, bypassed the apartment door and came up to the floor Sarah and Nala just vacated. She looked suspiciously around and up through the stair well. Then, went back down and entered the apartment. Azur stayed for about ten minutes, then, came out again. Sarah watched her amble down the street and go on another bus.

"Let's go quickly inside, and get what we need. You watch the window this time."

Sarah put Davida on the bed and went to the storeroom to retrieve her duffle bag. The only thing she still needed to do was to pack the baby's clothes. She had already changed into her Antarean uniform.

Suddenly, there was a panicky whisper from Nala, "Ras al Khazim just drove up in his car. What are we going to do?"

"Don't panic Nala. We're going to be okay." Sarah looked at her watch. The Explorer should be overhead by now. She opened com channel. "Explorer, this is Sarah, can you hear me?"

"Yes Sarah. Give us five more minutes and we will be within beam-up range."

"Okay Yoshi. Keep tracking."

Nala let out a wail. Al Khazim had come into the room followed by a woman who immediately went to the bed where Davida was sleeping.

"Ah, there are my two truants," Ras said in a honeyed voice. "What do you think you are doing?" he asked, and pointed to the duffle bag.

"Packing my Dear," Sarah replied in the same sugar coated tone.

"Ah, but where do you think you are going?"

"Home, my love."

Suddenly, the woman let out a screech. "Devil eyes, the baby has devil eyes," she shrieked, and dropped it back on the bed. Davida had awakened hearing voices, and let out a cry after being dropped. The woman turned on Ras. "No one will want her. Who do you think will buy a female with such weird eyes?"

Sarah turned on Ras. But he side stepped Sarah and picked up Davida, who with her PSI awareness recognized him immediately as a threat, and began to wail.

"Whose child is this? This is not Meshab's."

"Of course not," Sarah told him.

Ras turned toward the woman. "Leave now," he told her. When the door closed behind her, he turned on Sarah. "You stupid fool! You ruined everything." When he grabbed Davida by her heels and acted like he was about to slam the baby against the wall, Sarah screamed, "Yoshi help, help, Yoshi," and launched herself at Ras.

When Yoshi materialized in the room, Ras stared open-mouthed at him like he was an apparition. Nala screamed.

Yoshi pointed to the phaser, "This is a weapon, "he explained in a reasonable tone of voice, "and if you don't put that baby down, gently, I will kill you."

Before Ras could comply with the order, Sarah grabbed Davida from him, then, reached for Nala's hand. "Come, stand close to me and shut your eyes, don't move a muscle until I tell you," she told Nala. The last thing Sarah did was to scoop up her duffle bag.

"Energize," Yoshi said, and within a second, all four materialized on Scout I.

"Where's the Explorer?" Sarah asked, surprised.

"The scenario is, if Raz says you were kidnapped, the Explorer is able to deny any involved, and have no idea where you are."

"Oh, a political move?"

"No, Sarah Love, a legal one. We were in contact with Sargon, and he told us what to do."

"I see." Taking hold of the dazed Nala, she pulled her along the passageway to the bridge. "Hi Benjie, I'm glad you're in on it."

"Well, we Antareans need to stick together."

"Let's get out of Madras' space," Yoshi said. "After that, we can have a reunion on the Antares."

"How long will it take us to get there?"

"Only a second, Sarah."

"Yoshi now!" Pointing to the orange tips on the collar of her tunic which was the only thing denoting higher or command rank on the Antares she said, "I don't mind jokes. But right now I'm not very receptive."

Yoshi only gave her a perfunctory smile. "Yes Doctor, but right now I'm in command of Scout I. What I need you to do is to cover the children's eyes and lie on the floor, face down. When you hear a bell, you will close your eyes tight, and don't move. When you hear the bell chime twice you can get up, but not before. Got it?"

"Yes sir Yoshi. But why?"

"Like Sabrina explained it to me, if you want your world go out of focus, you can watch."

"Come, let's take care of the kids," Benjie said, as he rose from the navigation console.

While Yoshi programmed in the course for the Antares, Benjie talked softly to Nala and told her why she needed to cover her eyes. At first she wasn't cooperative, but when she saw Sarah doing the same to Davida, she finally agreed. Benjie laid down beside Nala, and tucked her close to his body. When the alarm sounded, Yoshi left his seat and hit the floor.

At first, Sarah could feel the normal vibration of the ship. This intensified as the computer took over, and as the ship accelerated, the vibrations became faster and rhythmic. Then, there was no sound, or sensation. When the Scout decelerated, sound and sensations were coming back, and a feeling that the ship was slowing down. When the bell chimed twice, Yoshi was off the floor.

Sarah rose more slowly. She uncovered Davida's eyes while Benjie pulled Nala into a sitting position, taking the cover off. When Sarah looked through the port-hole, the Antares loomed like a gigantic sphere out of the dark of space.

"Antares, this is Scout I, permission to dock."

"Scout I, this is the Antares, permission granted."

"Who was that?" Sarah asked.

"I don't know. I didn't recognize the voice either."

After docking, they all piled into the elevator and rode up to the bridge. Nala looked surprised when the car went first up, then sideways, and then straight again. When the doors to the bridge opened, only Android One and Charlie were manning the stations.

"Who's the Captain?" Yoshi asked.

"Commander Karsten, but he is in the bridge simulator," Android One answered.

"And where in thundration is that?" Sarah asked.

"Reenter the lift and I will have it stop at the proper level," Charlie told them, very familiar with human expressions.

The bridge simulator was something new. All three were eager to find out what it was all about. When the lift stopped and the doors opened, they all looked askance. It was a smaller version of the real bridge. Cadets were manning the stations.

Suddenly, Sarah gave a gasp. "What in the world is that?" she said, pointing to Karsten

Karsten shook his head. "Just as bad as Sabrina," he said, and chortled.

A second chuckle erupted and Sargon came forward. "Well hello," he said, and pointed to the hammock sling, "Sack of potatoes?" he asked

Sarah laughed and handed him the sling. "No, your daughter."

Sargon unzipped it and carefully lifted his daughter out. There was a happy gurgle from Davida as she felt herself freed from the encumbering net.

Nala, already fearful of the bewildering surroundings, became apprehensive when Sarah handed Davida to this strange looking giant of a man. Before he could settle himself on the floor to get acquainted with his daughter, Nala walked up to him and snatched the baby away.

Sargon looked at her surprised. "I'm not going to hurt her." Noticing the look of disbelief, he gently touched her hand. "No one will ever hurt you here," he told her soothingly in Galactic. A slight mind- meld took the fear of him away, and he also picked up her name. "Nala, look at my eyes. They are the same as Davida's. I'm her daddy."

"That won't wash," Sarah told him. "I brought you some literature from Madras. You should have acquainted yourself with their customs. Especially about women."

"I know. I found out, but too late for you. I started to put a resolution through the Alliance Counsel, so what happened to you will never happen to anyone else," Sargon told Sarah. Turning to Nala, "Can I have Davida now?"

Nala gave Sarah a questioning look.

"It's okay Nala. I wouldn't give him Davida if he wasn't nice," she assured the girl.

Reluctantly, Nala handed Davida to Sargon.

"Thank you Nala," he said, and commenced to bond with his daughter.

Sarah watched, then, somewhat impatient said, "I would like to go home now."

Sargon looked at her, then over at Karsten. Both started to laugh, remembering Sabrina's incensed reaction when she found she was homeless. Sargon rose and went to the com. When it was answered, "Ayhlean," he said, "I have Sarah here, and she needs temporary quarters."

"Okay. Bring her to my office."

"What you do mean, temporary quarters? Where's my apartment?"

"It has disappeared. Where your apartment was, now is an academy to train cadets. I noticed you scanned the kids when you came in…"

"And they're all strangers," Sarah interrupted.

"I opened the Antares as a training ground for space cadets."

"But why?"

"Someone has to earn money, to support all this."

"Has it ever occurred to you, that when someone comes home, they would like to find it the same as when they left?"

"Ditto," Yoshi added.

"Karsten, you think he's ready to take over?" Sargon asked, and pointed to Yoshi.

"Well, he's got to start sometime." Then reverting to Galactic he said, "Lieutenant Omi Hireyoshi, you have the bridge."

A little taken aback Yoshi answered, "I have the bridge," and it almost sounded like a question.

When Yoshi looked at Benjie, there was a wicked grin on Benjie's face, plus he was rubbing his hands as he looked at the cadets. Yoshi immediately got the drift and grinned back.

Poor kids, Sarah thought, remembering Yoshi's exacting command style.

Chapter 8

The last glow of the sinking sun still warmed lady Thalia's garden where Sabrina sat reading in a wicker chair. She laid the book down and stole a glance at Logan, now five months old, sleeping peacefully. A brief, but sad smile touched her face as she recalled nearly losing him to a difficult and dangerous pregnancy. Unbeknownst to her, Sargon's blood type had been incompatible with hers.

Shortly after Logan's birth, she and Chantar had left the Chateau and moved into an apartment in Port City, thus avoiding the ferocious storms and mountainous snow drifts of winter. In Port City, Sabrina reenrolled at The Academy to finish her law degree. Fortunately, she had found the law tapes in her duffle bag while on the Trefayne. Studying them had enabled her to test out of several classes and she successfully completed her bar-exam. She was now a full-fledged interstellar lawyer.

Then, three weeks ago Chantar relinquished the lease on her apartment in Port City and left with Sargon, but not before urging Sabrina to move back to the House of Sandor. Sabrina finally agreed to stay with Thalia as a guest until she could arrange transportation back to the Antares.

Sabrina heard footsteps advancing on the gravel, but she paid little attention to it, expecting it to be Tomas bringing her evening meal.

"I hope you enjoyed the warm day, Sabrina," Lady Lahoma said.

Surprised, Sabrina looked up. "Well, what's the special occasion? I thought Tomas was to take care of this," she said, and pointed to the tray Lady Lahoma was carrying.

"I'd like to have a chat with you."

"I don't know; your friendly chats are suspect," Sabrina teased.

"What a suspicious mind you have?"

"Experience."

Lahoma laughed. "Yes, naturally I have something on my mind. Otherwise, I wouldn't disturb your pleasant rest. I need you to take command of the Araxes."

"I thought this was to be Chiara's ship."

"It would have been, but she had to marry this...this male."

"What male?"

"Oh, you don't know? That's right, you haven't been back on the Antares. Chiarra married your Benjie," she said, and gave Sabrina a poisonous look.

"She did what?" Sabrina almost shouted she was so astonished. She propelled herself from the chair, but with enough presence to refrain from grabbing Lahoma by the shoulders. It seemed such a long time ago since Benjie had fallen head over heels in love with Chiara. It had been during their brief encounter on the Antares. Sabina's shout had awakened Logan, and he began to cry.

"See what you've done now? You woke the baby up," Lahoma scolded her.

Sabrina bent down and picked up Logan, cuddling him close. She looked down at his black downy head, then, her brow puckered. With a shrug she turned to Lahoma. "As much as I'd like to go, but as you see, I can't," she said holding the child out to Lahoma.

"You can take Logan with you." Lahoma waived him off and only patted his head. "The Araxes also carries passengers, so I think the two of you can be made quite comfortable. The Alliance has chartered the Araxes to take the Ambassador of Khitan back home. Since you know their language, I don't see any difficulty."

"Lahoma, do you know Thalon warned me about you?"

Lahoma only chuckled. "Then you will take the Araxes?"

"Since I can take Logan, I see no reason why not."

* * *

A few days later Sabrina left Logan in the care of Tomas, and was driven in a horse carriage out to the space port. After she arrived, she boarded a small hovercraft to transport her to where the ship was. The

Araxes, looking like a giant airplane was still sitting outside the hangar where Chiara had left it. Out in space, its wings retracted, and the Araxes became a spaceship.

Lady Lahoma informed Sabrina that she had ordered a complete overhaul after Chiara parked it and left with Benje. Benjie, at that time, had been teaching on Acheron. After the two met again, they decided to get married. Naturally, it was over Lahoma's protestation, but her granddaughter proven her match in stubbornness.

Sabrina's intention was to give the ship a pre-flight inspection, and to confer with the crew. Mardel would act as her co-pilot. His sister Kendra, and to her surprise, Joran was to accompany them also. Mardel and Kendra were Lady Lahoma's grandchildren by Rosana.

When Sabrina walked up to the ship, she found the hatch open, but no crew. She climbed in and then let herself down into the hold. The majority of the ship's belly was cargo space. She studied the still empty space and measured to see if there was room to stow the furniture she had collected over the years. Sabrina had decided that, immediately after this trip, to return to the Antares and have Mardel take the Araxes back to Acheron. Also, she wanted to see if the pay load that had to be picked up later on would fit. The hold was divided into two sections, a wide chamber with took almost a third of the ship, and a smaller one to store the passengers luggage, and whatever else they wanted to bring along.

Back on the bridge, she told the computer, "Systems report."

"Guidance system is functional. Communication system is functional. Weapons system is functional ..."

"Computer, continue systems check, then, log it," Sabrina said quickly, or she would hear the whole list in minute detail.

Again outside, she crawled up into the engine compartment and began checking the engines. Whoever done the overhaul, had done a thorough job. Easing herself down from the compartment, she sat on the tarmac, wiping her hands when she felt the hair at the back of her neck bristle. She had the distinct feeling of having an audience, and being scanned.

"Captain Hennesee?" a woman's questioning voice asked in Galactic. Before she could turn, the woman's companion said, "Sabrina?"

"Elkatma n' el Halim, what a pleasure to see you again," Sabrina said. She remembered the Chiron Ambassador from the party she had attended. It seemed such a long time ago. She had also met him several times afterwards in the company of Lady Thalia, and that seemed like a long time ago too.

"Sabrina, let me introduce Talimar na' el Halim, my consort."

"I'm very pleased to meet you Talimar na' el Halim," Sabrina returned in the Chiron's language.

"My pleasure," Talimar said politely, trying to scan Sabrina, but immediately felt a wall go up at her most delicate touch. Apparently she has PSI abilities. Interesting creature. Her son Estel seemed to be interested in her, and held her in respect, Talimar mused. Even after the way she walked off his ship. Then there was the sudden relinquishing of her command of the Trefayne. After all this, and the other illogical behavior, yet Elkatma thought highly of her. She was intrigued. Her consort's regard was sparingly given.

Suddenly there was the wail of an infant. "I was just going to fire up the engines to check their performance. I guess this has to wait," Sabrina said, and sighed.

Joran came toward her, carrying Logan. It was his time to be nursed. Joran's mouth twitched when he said, "His lordship is demanding your attention," and handed the baby to her.

She took Logan from him who immediately began to pull on her coveralls. "You impatient imp," she said, and turned to Elkatma and Talimar, "As you can see, I need to be excused. Let me introduce you to Joran Sandor ra Hennesee. He will give you a tour of the ship and show you where to stow your things. He can answer all your questions. I will join you later."

* * *

Next morning, with Logan riding comfortable in his hammock slung over her shoulder, Sabrina returned to the space port and arrived at the same time as the Ambassador and his wife.

"We only need for the catering service to start loading. Joran will take care of that. Do you wish to board the ship?" she asked Elkatma and Talimar

"We are in no hurry," Elkatma n' el Halim said. "Three days will be enough time to get familiar with the ship."

Suddenly, the sling erupted as Logan grunted and stretched. He had awakened and immediately wanted out. As soon as the sling was unzipped, his head popped out and he squirmed to look around. When Elkatma saw his eyes, astonishment clearly registered on the Chiron's face. "Captain Thalon's child?" he asked.

Talimar regarded mother and child, intrigued by this new development.

It took some effort for Sabrina to refrain from smiling when she said, "Yes."

"But, I thought he was married to Chantar Bahrain ra Sandor?" Elkatma said

"He is." Then Sabrina smiled. "But that was sometime after I claimed house-rights." When Elkatma looked uncomprehendingly at her, she relented and explained, "I also carry the name ra Thalon, Sargon's house name. Any female member of his house who is not related by blood, or in any other way, can claim the right to bear his child so the line or name won't die out." she told him.

Elkatma fell silent, never having heard of anything like this before. But then, he was not conversant with the Antarean culture. When he thought back, Captain Thalon had been exceedingly uncommunicative about the circumstances surrounding the Antareans. Still pondering what Sabrina had told him, he gave Talimar a raised eyebrow as both stepped aside to make room as the caterers began loading.

While Joran began instructing the caterers in how and where to stow the food, Sabrina lazily watched the traffic around her. Suddenly she stiffened. To her utter disbelieve, she saw Machir Aram coming toward the Araxes.

When he saw her, he abruptly stopped. Sabrina surmised he expected to see Chiara. As he came closer, his strides became a strut. His whole body posture became a blatant display of his cocky attitude. A woman, contrary to Acheron's custom, was following several steps behind. It was also very apparent that she was pregnant. When he was close enough, and certain that he had Sabrina's attention, he reached back and pulled the woman forward until she was leaning against his body. With a supercilious grin he ran his hand over her swollen belly.

Why, he's flaunting her pregnancy, Sabrina thought astonished, and then felt irked.

As soon as Joran caught sight of the spectacle, he mumbled incensed, "Like always, he can't leave well enough alone," and wondered what this was all about. He tried to step in front of Sabrina.

"No Joran," Sabrina told him, holding him back. She handed him the baby with, "Take care of Logan." Clenching her fists and her body taunt, she slowly advanced toward Machir Aram.

When Machir Aram saw her move toward him, some of his cockiness evaporated. His eyes began to dart between Sabrina and Joran. An uneasy feeling began to grow in the pit of his stomach, and he wondered why he had come back. Sabrina's whole stance was a threat. His mouth was going dry as he watched her lips draw back into a feral grin.

"You think, because I said nothing to Lahoma you would get away with what you've done to me?" Her voice was harsh, as her startling sea-green eyes bore into him. Suddenly she whirled, and her right foot impacted viciously against Machir Aram's chest.

As he went down the woman screamed. Joran rushed to her side to pull her out of harm's way.

Machir Aram rolled and came up just a fraction too slow as Sabrina hit him double fisted in the face. He was not unaccustomed to fighting, having been in brawls before, winning most of them. He gathered himself, using his fury against the pain, he aimed for her face. Sabrina effortlessly side-stepped as he tried to punch her. He was not prepared for Sabrina's disciplined mode of attack. When she moved in, Joran knew Machir Aram had no chance. Sabrina was a trained warrior, needing no weapon. She was a weapon. Her early training in Karate had been augmented by Sargon's extensive knowledge of the martial arts.

When Mardel and his sister arrived, both waded in and tried to stop the fight. It took their combined strength to pull Sabrina off.

"Sabrina, lay off, you're killing him," Mardel shouted into her ear.

Sabrina heard him and finally ceased. She was breathing hard as she looked at Machir Aram lying at her feet. She grabbed him by his hair and pulled him into a half sitting position. She looked at the woman. "Do you understand Kreala?" she asked. When the woman nodded, Sabrina looked to Joran, and then at Kendra and Mardel, "You are my witnesses." Pointing to Machir Aram, she said, "You see this male? This male, he is mine."

The woman stood motionless, not comprehending as she stared at Sabrina.

"Mardel, call an air-cab and have them both taken to Lahoma." Sabrina ordered.

Machir Aram tried to raise a hand, it moved agonizingly slow. "No Mardel," erupted from his swollen lips. "I want to go to my mother; I want to go to Port City." His words were barely understandable.

Sabrina, still breathing hard, gave him a pensive look. She understood him well. He did not care to face his grandmother, the indomitable matriarch of the House of Sandor without the support of his mother. She also knew there would be no escape for him, sooner or later he would have to face Lahoma.

"You will see Lahoma, and you will explain to the House of Sandor what you have done to me."

Defeated, Machir Aram crumbled to the tarmac.

Mardel standing in Araxes' door reported "The air-cab is on its way."

Within five minutes the air-cab landed, Sabrina told the driver to take his fare to the House of Sandor, giving him the address. Then, turned to Mardel, "Is everything ready?"

"Yes, Sir."

"Good, let's get this show underway. Mardel, go and start the engines." Turning to Elkatma and Talimar, "I'm sorry you were subjected to this. This was a debt he owed me," Sabrina told them.

"What will happen to the woman?" Talimar na el Halim asked.

"She will be alright. I doubt Lady Lahoma will move against Machir Aram until my return." Noting the intrigued look on Talimar's face, she quickly said, "We better get inside before we have to breath the engine's exhaust." She led the Ambassador and his wife up the ramp and toward the passenger compartments. "Kendra will see to that you are comfortable," she told them.

Sabrina manually piloted the Araxes until it hit Mach I, then the computer took over. She left the pilot's seat, turning control over to Mardel, and went to take a shower. While in the shower, she tried to let the water calm her so she could at least face Logan. She knew he became distressed when he picked up the whole gamut of her emotions. She emerged to see Joran sitting on her bed, holding Logan on his lap.

"Now, will you tell me what this was all about," he demanded. "Logan became so upset, I had to leave."

Sabrina winced. "You will know when the House of Sandor knows," she told him. She retrieved Logan, who was still agitated, first to sooth him and then to nurse him.

Joran swallowed his temper with difficulty. "Why won't you tell me?" With a probing gaze he tried to penetrate the wall she had put up. "You won't, or can't?" he finally asked.

"Both."

* * *

Sabrina was in the cockpit watching the computer read out, and she was also playing with Logan, when Talimar walked in.

"Am I interrupting?'

"No, there is nothing going on."

Talimar tried to be tactful, but she had so many questions. Having never dealt with an Antarean, she found it difficult to decide on an approach. A small smile curved her lips upwards as she asked, "Is your life always that eventful?"

Sabrina frowned. "You mean the fight?"

"Elkatma said your style was superb and very effective."

"Not my favorite pastime."

Talimar softly cleared her throat. She regarded Sabrina for a moment, then, decided on a direct approach. "Have you lived long on Acheron?"

"I lived there only long enough to fulfill a requirement." Noting Talimar's puzzled look, Sabrina relented. "I was sent to Acheron to attend the Space Academy. It is a requirement to join the Alliances Star Fleet. Lady Thalia ra Sandor was my sponsor."

"This was my first time to visit Acheron. I'm a cultural scientist, and an anthropologist. I was very fascinated by the technological development on Acheron."

Sabrina smiled. "You mean the anachronisms you observed."

"Yes. It was intriguing. Naturally, I asked many questions, but received few answers.

"I'm sure you are aware of Acheron's history."

"Yes. I observed the many houses that are still empty. The population is only now slowly recovering from the ravages of war, and especially the pollution. I also learned that there are still prevailing genetic damages."

"The wars ended a century ago. Many of the families have never recovered, and died out. The House of Sandor is still dealing with this tragedy. They learned the hard way that a nation prospers under peace and is decimated by wars."

"I had great difficulty with the government of Acheron disclosing the extent of the damages, and to get acquainted with their social customs and mores. I know the society is matriarchal. Their government is well run and they have an excellent police force, and very little crime."

"Most squabbles are settled within the families. If another house is involved it is settled between the matriarchs of those houses. Their word is law."

"Couldn't this become an abuse of power?" Talimar asked.

"No. If the contention is serious, an arbitrator is present, or the courts will intervene. I have studied their laws, and there are very few loopholes."

"And your contention with the man Machir Aram?"

"Talimar!" Elkatma exclaimed from the door. He had walked into the cockpit some time ago and listened in on the discourse.

"Elkatma, if I don't ask, how will I ever get answers?" Turning to Sabrina she said, "You see, I have been offered a job as a cultural attaché after I finish my doctorate. I have decided to do my thesis on the cultural differences between a patriarchy and a matriarchy."

"That's a tall order, Talimar," Sabrina told her.

"I discovered that, after I came to Acheron. I ran into a wall of silence where family is concerned. I noted that you carry the house name of Sandor and wondered if the man Machir Aram is your husband?"

A thin smile curved Sabrina's mouth as she looked at Talimar. "He was, but he is no longer. There was a contract of marriage, dissolved if I left Acheron. I have left Acheron some time ago."

Elkatma raised an eyebrow. "But after your fight, you claimed Machir Aram."

"I claimed the right to Machir Aram. That is all."

"What will you do when you return to Acheron?"

"Elkatma, he wronged me and he paid for it. When I return to Acheron, I will give him back to his mother, and she can do with him as she pleases."

"And the pregnant woman?"

"I will claim the child, but return it to the mother so both will have a place in the House of Sandor. It is Machir Aram's child and so should remain within the family."

"Are you paying Lahoma back for what she did to you?"

Sabrina's eyebrows went up as she looked at Elkatma. "So Sargon has talked to you about it?"

"Yes, I asked him after I met you at that party. Your maneuvering had not escaped me."

Sabrina laughed. "Elkatma you are very observant and I think very conversant with the laws of Acheron."

"As an Ambassador, I have to be."

Logan tired of playing with his mother's fingers had fallen asleep. Sabrina looked down at the child and said. "He's ready for bed now." She called Kendra and after she came, gave the baby to her.

"Then what is your relationship with Joran Sandor?" Talimar asked. "I naturally noted your familiarity with him."

"You are inquisitive Talimar," Sabrina said.

"Naturally, it is important for me to learn, and I can do that only if I ask questions. On Acheron there is a reticence about discussing the intimate relationships within families."

Sabrina looked at Talimar and nodded her head. "I understand the wall you must have run up against. Joran is the son of Lahoma and Radamas. He has joined my house of his own free will. This means he is free to leave or stay. He is neither obligated, nor bounded to me."

"You have learned Acheron's reticence," Elkatma told her.

"Even where I come from, some things are private." This was said in a tone that was clearly dismissive.

Chapter 9

As the Araxes entered the Hyades, Sabrina cut down on the brilliant light of Khitan's sun by dimming the screen. Logan slept across her knees, his chest rising and falling with his rhythmic breathing. Gently, she put him into the hammock sling and fastened it securely into the wall. Then she began the approach sequence, reducing speed to mach three, then two, then one. When the ship closed in on Khitan, the Chiron home world, Sabrina called Elkatma to the bridge to contact the tower for landing permission. He took the ear phone and soon turned to Sabrina, "We have permission to land."

"Okay, let's start decent. Landing procedure," she informed her crew, then ordered everyone to strap in." Having ascertained which landing strip, she expertly brought the space craft in. After disembarking, Elkatma and Talimar were met by Estel in a car and taken home. Sabrina didn't even get a change to say hello to her former Captain. Then, she hadn't expected it.

* * *

At the Space Port they went through refurbishing the craft, taking on fresh water and an exchange of air. Sabrina was just checking the air pressure when a well known voice behind her said, "So, you're piloting Lady Lahoma's ships now."

"Hello, Captain Estel n el Halim. No, this is just a one time favor. I have no desire to become a space taxi for dignitaries, or shuttle cargo. What brings you here?"

"When my parent's told me who their pilot was, I thought to come and say hello."

"That's very nice of you, but not a typical Chiron behavior."

"What you are trying to say is that you didn't expect me to acknowledge your presence here? Then, for my not so typical behavior you can thank Ian for it. Earth people are a bad influence."

"That's what Captain Thalon found out after he became involved with us."

Estel looked her up and down, weighing his next question, "Why the outburst on my ship?"

"Captain, that's a long story. It was a contention between Captain Thalon and myself. It had nothing to do with you. But you had your crew intact; I didn't see the need for you to have an extra ensign."

"Was your pride hurt because you didn't have an important position?"

"No, it was an opportunity to pay Captain Thalon back for his authoritarian behavior. Like I said, it's a long story."

"How is the child?'

"He is doing fine."

"He is Captain Thalon's?"

"Yes, why all the curiosity?"

Estel looked at her, then raised his hand in departure and said, "Sabrina, a long life and happiness." But before he left he handed her a computer disc. "Commander Dan asked me to give this to you." He gave Joran a nod as he passed.

"Sabrina, what was all that about?"

"If I knew, I would tell you," she said, still taken aback by the unexplained visit, and then the mysterious questions. "Are we about ready to take off?"

"Yes. We've finished taking on water. Everything is disconnected from the ship. That was what I came to tell you."

"Where are Mardel and Kendra?"

"They went to a shop to buy something. Ah there they are. Mardel what have you been up to?"

We bought some fresh fruits. Are we ready for take off?"

"Yes. Give this stuff to Kendra, and let's get ready," Sabrina told Mardel. "Tower, this is the Araxes, asking permission for take off."

"Araxes, you are cleared on runway nine. Start departure, now."

"Joran get everything ready for take off. Mardel take navigation."

Sabrina taxied to runway nine, and lined the ship up for takeoff. Back in space, she left Mardel in control of the cockpit and went to see how Logan was faring. She found him securely tied in his crib, and sound asleep.

"Our next destination is Cassandra's world to get the Zirbelnuts, then, home to the Antares," she told Joran.

The Zirbelnuts came from Sargon's home world. Since it was not practical to have large animals on the Antares, the nuts were an excellent source of protein. The nuts were generally ground into powder and loaded into the food-replicator. The powder was bland, but when properly seasoned, could be made to taste like anything. Sabrina and her friends usually made them into shakes tasting like vanilla, chocolate, strawberries, or whatever their hearts desired. Also pot-roast could be reconstituted from the powder, or even the taste of liver, but naturally it hadn't been the girls favorite.

Cassandra, who grew them for commercial use, had received a requisition from Lahoma, and for Sabrina to deliver the cargo to a space station.

* * *

While enrout to Cassandra's world, Sabrina opened the disc Dan had given to Estel. Dan thought she would be interested in the outcome of their findings. His style was succinct and gave only the major points.

It began: Sabrina greetings. I thought you would be interested in the outcome of this scientific endeavor. We found many more layers of civilization, but had to evacuate as a precaution after we discovered why the people and their planet died. In one of their temples we found a collection of platinum discs, carefully preserved in airtight containers. After some modification to our computers we were able to read them. It took time, but we were finally able to decipher their language. The people called themselves the Santals and their language Orija. By Khitan standard, they were an ancient civilization that had developed a technology beyond what we now understand. The early Santals seem to have led colorful and eventful lives. They conquered space a long time ago and appeared to have been adventurous. We found many legends and stories pertaining to their exploits. But our interests mostly centered on unraveling their extensive technology, which according to some of their writing, a major part was lost to cataclysmic events.

Religion appeared in every part of their life. The Santals believed that gods and goddesses took part in every human activity from birth to death. They believed the laws to issue directly from the gods. The reason we never found any portraits of the people, was because their religion forbade producing images of man, animal, or fauna. All life was considered sacred and animated by spirit. Also they did not bury their dead, but cremated instead. We noticed several abrupt divisions between their civilizations. The discs revealed that great cataclysms devastated the whole planet at different intervals. Much of their older knowledge was completely lost. For ages, physical survival had been the basic need. After every cataclysm, technology and their civilization seemed to have taken a downward drift. It was in their last epoch that they became builders of machines, like cars, trains, tanks, earth moving machine's, you name them. Also it was in this time period when they loosened the scourge of the spores as they called it.

Now we come to what caused the planets decimation. It began with overpopulation. To make room for a land hungry population, they invaded the rain forests, cutting down its trees. But unbeknown to them, they stirred up a fungus which proved to be their nemesis. At first the death only appeared in small clusters, but later spread out among the populace. For a while they thought it contained. But then another outbreak occurred, spreading in an ever widening circle, decimating the population. It was when they decided to build their cities underground. You remember the one we found?

The last disc described how for hundreds of years they lived safely down in their cities. Thinking the fungus had died out, they again moved topside, and began to reclaim the land. At first, all went well. It was during that time they built the city we found inside the canyon. They thought that moisture, or a certain level of water saturation, reactivated the spores. The symptoms of the spore infection was a rise in body temperature, followed by apathy, eventually the lungs filled with fluid. They drowned in their own body fluids. I hope this satisfies some of your curiosity. If you like to have more information, come and visit Khitan. Wishing you a long life and happiness. Dan.

Chapter 10

It took four weeks to reach the vicinity of Cassandra's home. The course was correct, but her world seemed to have disappeared. Sabrina laid in a search pattern to find it.

Cassandra's world was bizarre; it was a life-form that grew. Also, Cassandra, as Sabrina discovered was strange. The first time they met, Cassandra had taken an active dislike to her. And it was not out of generosity when she gave Sabrina a small spaceship now called Spitfire.

To kill time while they searched for Cassandra's world, Sabrina worked with the on-board computer, refining the blue print for her villa. Joran, looking over her shoulder asked, "What is that?" pointing to the diagram of an octagonal cell.

"That my dear, is my nursery cell. And here are the blue prints of my Roman villa."

"What's a Roman villa?"

"Joran, that's hard to explain. You see I had a grandfather who was Italian…"Looking up at Joran, she saw his blank expression, "I guess this won't make much sense to you. I'm building my villa in the ancient style of his country. And these are the blueprints."

"The place you will live in?"

"Yes, now go and let me work until Logan wakes up."

Logan had grown steadily; he was now almost eight months old. Since the Chirons left, there was little for the crew to do, so Logan was being royally spoiled. He was crawling all over the place, and Sabrina could already see that he was developing into an imp.

Suddenly, the computer interrupted Sabrina's calculation for the floor plan. The sensors had detected Cassandra's world. It was slowly drifting through space to nowhere, and it had grown some more since Sabrina had last seen it.

"Cassandra, this is Sabrina, may we come along side?"

"Sabrina? Where is Chiara?"

Sabrina, affecting a teasing tone said, "Chiara found herself a sweetheart, and absconded to the Antares."

A chuckle came over the speaker. "Well, I guess that's all right. I have the nuts ready for you to pick up. Why don't you come over and visit me while the others are doing the loading."

Sabrina was taken aback by the friendly invitation. She remembered Miri's warning that Cassandra could be very dangerous and unpredictable. Nevertheless she said, "Okay, I'll see you in a few minutes." Sabrina brought the Araxes along side and had a long tube interfacing from her ship to Cassandra's world. She told Joran and Kendra to get the cargo loaded as quickly as possible. Then she asked Mardel to stay at the controls and beam her back at the slightest sign of trouble.

The interior of Cassandra's world gave Sabrina an eerie feeling. It felt like walking though the insides of a living creature. The rumbling she heard reminded her too much of a growling stomach. The walls around her gave off an iridescent light; it almost suggested fireflies back on Earth. She held Logan close to her body, her arms securely wrapped around him. In her path, a small rivulet came bubbling out of the ground, flowing toward a patch of grassland ahead. There were trees looking like Aspen and Birch. Sabrina let out a sigh of relief when she espied the grass and trees ahead. This was the area she remembered from her first visit.

Cassandra came toward her, but stopped, when she saw the child. When she held out her hands, Sabrina smiled and handed Logan to her. But then, to her horror Cassandra's mouth opened, its outline becoming blurred; it looked like she was going to devour him. Terrified, Sabrina started to grab for him, but when Cassandra saw Logan's eyes, her mouth clamped shut. "Thalon's?" she asked surprised.

"Yes Cassandra, this is Thalon's son. I wanted to introduce him to you." It took all of her willpower not to snatch the baby back. Instead, Sabrina carefully shielded her thoughts and only smiled.

Cassandra held the baby over her head and wriggled his stout little body back and forth, much to Logan's amusement. "How is Thalon?" she asked.

"I don't know. I haven't seen him."

"He and Chantar were here and brought books and computer discs."

"I have Lady Lahoma's pay voucher," Sabrina said, wanting to cut her stay short, handing it to Cassandra.

"Why don't you keep it and deposit it to my account at the Space Station."

"I can do that. I think I better get back to the ship," Sabrina said, taking Logan from her she turned to leave.

"Sabrina?" When Sabrina turned back toward her, Cassandra's eyes were scanning her. "Do you love Thalon?"

"Why do you ask?"

"You have his child."

"Cassandra, Thalon is unique in this galaxy. I claimed house rights to perpetuate his genes." Only too late did Sabrina realize this was not what Cassandra wanted to hear.

Cassandra's wide open eyes contracted and she looked like a cat about to spring. "So when he dies..."

"Cassandra," Sabrina interrupted, "before Thalon dies, I will be long dead."

"I don't know, I don't know," Cassandra murmured.

"Why don't you tell me what you are getting at?"

In an instant Cassandra's russet eyes changed to orange, the movements of her lithe body reminded Sabrina of a snake about to strike. There was a hiss escaping from her clenched teeth.

"Cassandra!" The voice was couched in a tone of warning, and it came from Lara.

Sabrina and Cassandra spun around. Lara seemed to have appeared from nowhere, and was walking toward them with her easy rolling gait."

"I smell a tinge of smoke in the air. Have you two been sparing?" Lara asked Cassandra. "Why don't you tell Sabrina about your vision?"

"Lara," the voice was a warning.

"Cassandra Love, if you don't, I will." Lara said.

Cassandra spun toward Sabrina with her finger pointing, "You," she said, "you…"

"Sabrina," Lara interrupted, "Cassandra had a vision of Thalon being surrounded by flames. In some way she thinks you're responsible for it. Cassandra's visions somehow always come true. In her mind you are the symbol of Thalon's destruction. She also has a phobic fear of fire.

"I see. I'm glad you told me because I could not imagine how I incurred Cassandra's enmity from my first meeting, because nothing happened between us." Turning to Cassandra, "Thalon means my life. Also, as you can see, he is the father of my son. I could never do anything to hurt Thalon. I don't know what your vision implies. Since I cannot see into the future, I have no answer to your vision." Sabrina was about to turn away, there was a hoarse and bewildered whisper from Cassandra, "But he was old, he was old."

Sabrina and Lara both stared at her. When Cassandra opened her eyes, she looked startled at Lara. "It never occurred to me, but when I just recalled the vision, for the first time I looked closer at Thalon, and he looked like an old man."

"Sabrina, I think it better if you leave. I will take care of Cassandra," Lara told her.

Sabrina turned and forced herself to walk slowly away. It took all her self-control not to run to get her son and herself away. Back on the Araxes she was silent and her mind preoccupied when she initiated starting sequences. Mardel tried to get her attention. She looked up at him, then, shuddered.

"I know," he said, "weird place. I just came to tell you that the Araxes is uncoupled from Cassandra's world.

"Good, let's go."

* * *

Four weeks later they arrived at the Space Station. After unloading the protein powder, Sabrina went to deposit the voucher into Cassandra's account. She was about to ask for the departure schedule, when she was informed that she had passengers. A Prince Sarum el Mashad, his two wives, and two children were to be taken to Voran, a planet within the Hyades.

At least it's taking us closer to home, and maybe the children could entertain Logan, Sabrina temporized. She returned to the Araxes to inform the others and to order more supplies and water for extra consumption.

Until now, there had been ample space on Araxes' top deck. There was room to exercise and play games. Sometimes, Kendra, using cushions, turned it into a place to socialize. She would often ask Sabrina to play her guitar while she accompanied her on her flute. For Logan who had just stared to find his legs, the area was large enough to move around and play with his toys. Now the crew's quarter was downsized into three cabins to accommodate the passengers.

Sabrina was just coming from the cockpit when Joran ushered the passengers on board. Both women were veiled. One of the women was leading a boy by the hand, and the man led the other boy.

"Prince Sarum el Mashad, welcome on board," Joran greeted him as they entered the ship.

Prince Sarum totally ignored him, his eyes glued on Sabrina as she came down the hallway. As usually she was dressed in her coverall. The exception this time was that she wore a wide belt, decorated with her asterics. He noted that she was taller than he, and somehow it irritated him. He fastened his malignant eyes on her, taking her measure, then, glanced at his two wives. His wives were diminutive and compliant, keeping their eyes downcast. Useless women, he thought, despising them. He hated women. In his estimate they were lower than animals; only good for breeding. But this female, with her commanding presence and easy stride, made him feel uncomfortable. He decided then and there to teach her, her place, to have her cowed. He had been in bad temper ever since he was unexpectedly ordered back to Voran; which bode ill. Being hostage to Mirko, king of Voran, had given him status and freedom he never experienced before. It also had been a respite, being away from his father, and the intrigues and machination of his very manipulative family.

Logan, now a little more than a year old, came crawling as fast as he could down the corridor, giggling with glee. He had slipped away from Kendra, and naturally, was getting in the way. Prince Sarum, using his boot, pushed Logan roughly aside.

Logan let out a protesting wail.

Enraged, Sabrina moved quickly to pick him up. "You will never do that again," she warned him.

"Where I come from, females do not talk, unless spoken to." he told her haughtily

"Where I come from, babies are special people. They are treated with consideration and love," she fired back.

"Silly woman," he said. His eyes first raked Mardel then stopped on Joran, who was the older male, and drawled, "I hope you will keep your females manageable," pointedly looking at Kendra, and then at Sabrina.

Joran's face went crimson, but Sabrina put a hand on his arm, shaking her head. She gave Logan to Kendra, then said, "Mardel, come with me to get the ship ready for departure." Sabrina turned on her heels and marched off with Mardel following her to the cockpit.

"It's going to be difficult living at close quarters with his coxcomb," Mardel remarked with a sour expression.

Later, Joran and Kendra poked their heads into the cockpit. "It's going to be as unpleasant as hell with this guy here," Kendra remarked. "What are we going to do?'

Kendra, you'll take care of the women, and Joran, I'm sorry, it's going to fall on you to keep this ninny placated. I'm going to stay as much as possible out of his way. Three weeks are not forever."

"But it's going to seem like it," Kendra said.

"I know, it's going to be a bitch," her brother agreed.

"I'll take the night shift," Sabrina told Mardel. "All of you have to keep an eye on Logan. Keep Logan out of his sight so this Prince can't repeat his offensive behavior."

* * *

For almost two weeks, all went well, and Sabrina never saw her passengers. It was getting toward the end of the third week, when Joran and Sabrina came down the corridor to check on an electrical short. Prince Sarum appeared at the door of his room to ask what the trouble was. Joran tried to obscure the prince's view of Sabrina by placing himself in front of her. "We just have an electrical short. It will be fixed immediately. So please go back to your cabin, there is nothing to worry about," he assured him.

Prince Sarum suddenly noticed Sabrina, and moved into the middle of the narrow corridor to block her way. By then, both wives, attracted by the noise, looked out of their door.

Sabrina walked up to him, but he just stood there unwilling to move. She looked straight into his eyes.

"Woman, lower your eyes," he commanded.

"Would you step aside so I can fix the electrical problem?" she asked.

The prince stood his ground, and with his wives watching, couldn't back down; his male pride wouldn't allow it.

Sabrina held her temper with difficulty and turning to Joran said, "Joran have this male moved."

With deliberate calm, Joran asked him, "Sir, please let the captain pass so she can fix the problem."

"What are you, a man or a mouse? Letting a woman tell you what to do!"

"Sir, the Lady is the captain and her orders must be obeyed." He gently pushed the Prince aside.

Sabrina went to fix the short. As she reached inside to straighten the wires, a spark hit her on the back of her hand. Startled, Prince Sarum let out a bellow. "See, she is a stupid cow," he yelled at Joran.

Both Joran and Sabrina ignored him. Also his wives, considered a retreat would be prudent, went back into their room.

From that day on, Prince Sarum vowed that in some way he would get even with Sabrina. He desired her; she aroused him like no other woman ever had. When those emerald eyes looked at him, the heat in his body increased. When she regarded him with impassive coldness, his lust for her swelled. She was beautiful, proud and willful, and he wanted to possess her. There was a need to make her responsive to his manhood. He thought of her day and night and, she even troubled his dreams.

* * *

Only three more days, Sabrina thought, as she left the cockpit to go to the galley. Logan was asleep in the crew cabin with Joran watching over him. As she walked up to the galley, Prince Sarum stood blocking the doorway, swaying back and forth on the balls of his heels. When

Sabrina stopped in front of him, he grinned, "Say pretty please," he demanded.

"Please, would you move aside?" she asked.

He laughed. "You have acquired manners, I see."

"Would you please move?"

Sarum grinned. He reached up and patted her cheek, then, his hand cupped her breast. "It behooves a pretty woman to be compliant and have manners."

Just at this moment, Mardel came from the crew quarters. It was close to a shift change, and for Sabrina to be relieved. Mardel was at least two inches taller and more broad-shouldered than the Prince.

Sabrina turned to Mardel, "Please move this male out of my way," she ordered, with her accent heavy on the male.

Prince Sarum's hand came up to slap Sabrina's face.

She parried and pinned his arm against the wall.

"Prince Sarum el Mashad, you are confined to your quarters for the rest of the journey. If you leave your quarters I will personally throw you in the brig. Do you understand me? Mardel, you will escort his highness to his quarters, and see to that he does not leave them."

"Aye, Sir. Your Highness, will you return to your quarters?"

The prince's temper flared, but instantly subsided, and he said nothing. He silently returned to his cabin without a look at Sabrina or Mardel.

In the galley, Sabrina made herself a strawberry protein drink, then, sat down with a feeling of disquiet. She had noticed the Prince's brooding mood and the way he watched her. Something about it troubled her. She grimaced and moved her head, trying to ease the tensions. She needed to be relaxed before Logan would demand her attention again. No use in transmitting her emotions through their bond and getting the baby upset. He was already fretting because the reduced quarters curtailed his activities. He was an active and inquisitive child and they all had to find new ways to keep him entertained.

* * *

The last three days passed without incident, and after the Araxes landed, Sabrina hoped that this would be the last she would ever see of Prince Sarum. Joran, just completed supervising the taking on of fresh supplies, kept checking the time. "What's keeping him so long?" he mumbled to himself. Mardel should have been back at least half an hour ago. The control tower had been hedging about their takeoff time. Mardel was sent to check on their status. With a worried frown on his face, Joran walked into the cockpit and checked off his inventory. Sabrina signed it. Just then Kendra strode through the door, "Mardel's not back yet?" she asked.

"No. And I'm getting concerned. Has he called in?" Joran asked Sabrina.

Sabrina sat at the controls, going through her check list for departure. "No, haven't heard from him yet."

"Hum, this is curious. I'll call the tower," Joran said, and went to the communication console, "Tower, this is the Acheron merchant vessel Araxes. Do we have takeoff time?"

"Araxes, this is the tower. We have a slight problem. There are several ships coming in. We pray for your indulgence."

"We are also looking for a Commander Mardel Sandor. He's supposed to have stopped by at your place."

"Tower. No one by that name stopped by here."

"Thank you tower. Araxes out."

While Joran talked to the tower, Kendra tried to raise Mardel on his communicator. She looked startled. "That's odd. It's turned off," she said

Sabrina slowly rose from her seat, still studying the read-out on the console. She looked at Kendra and then at Joran. "I've checked all the controls and everything is ready for take off. Logan will be asleep for sometime. I'll go and check on Mardel."

Sabrina had been gone for thirty minutes when Mardel walked in. In an angry voice he said, "I never heard of anything like it. I was stopped by two station police and they told me that my communicator was interfering with their transmission. They detained me and took it way from me. I don't know what they did to it."

"We wondered. You were out of communication for twenty minutes," Kendra told him. "Sabrina went to look for you."

"I didn't see her, where did she go?"

"She probably went to police headquarters."

"Let's wait fifteen more minutes then, try to contact her."

"No, I think we should contact her now," Joran said.

"Okay, might as well," Kendra agreed. She said the ship checks out, and we're ready for lift off as soon as we get clearance."

* * *

Sabrina crossed the airfield and walked down a passageway between two buildings toward police headquarters. Suddenly, she was ambushed from behind and a piece of cloth put over her mouth and nose. She struggled, but a fast acting narcotic rendered her immediately unconscious. When Sabrina came to, she was disoriented and felt queasy. Something covered her head and her hands and feet were tied. Remaining as motionless as possible, she listened. She could discern two or three voices, and they were talking in an unknown language. She also felt vibration through the floor and sensed motion, deciding she must be in some kind of motorized conveyance. Two people, men based from their voices, held her down with their feet on top of her.

At first the vehicle seemed to be traveling at a leisurely pace, but suddenly the speed picked up. For a while, the road was smooth, but soon became more uneven and bumpy. Sabrina felt like hours had gone by. Whatever covered her head was dusty and smelled unclean. Her throat was beginning to get parched. When the vehicle slowed down, Sabrina, in a whiny voice informed them, "I have to pee." Someone hit her with a sharp rap over the head. "If you don't let me out, I'll pee all over this place." The vehicle stopped and she was roughly pulled out. She desperately wanted that thing covering her head off so she stumbled and fell. "I can't see," she complained in the same whiny voice. After what sounded like a short conference, her head was freed and her hands and feet untied. She realized she had been stuffed into a sack. It was already dark, but she could see that the conveyance was a car. Three men, leaning against it, watched as she wobbled on still unsteady legs toward a small bush where she squatted to relieve herself. When she came back, her hands and feet were retied, but the sack was left off. She was unceremoniously pushed down to the floorboard in the back of the car.

* * *

The morning just dawned when the car finally stopped in front of a small castle. Again, she was roughly dragged out, and since her legs were still shaky, half carried down to a basement, where she was literally thrown into a cell. For a moment she lay on the floor, stunned. But as soon as the door closed, she began to work on the thongs that bound her hands and feet. She worked them steadily until she could feel a small give in the tightness. It didn't take long and she had the straps binding her wrists off, then, untied her feet. Getting up was difficult. She used the wall to prop herself up. Whatever the narcotic had been, it was still lingering in her system.

She went to investigate her cell. The walls were made of solid stone with no windows, and the door of iron-studded hardwood. The cell was escape-proof. Disheartened, she sank down on the floor with her back in a corner. Her stone-cell was bare. There wasn't even a bed or bench to sit on. The sanitary facility was a hole in the floor.

* * *

Sabrina had no concept of how much time had passed. But it felt like an eternity when an old woman came in bringing water and a slice of bread. When the woman entered, Sabrina heaved herself unsteadily into a sitting position. She had been lying on the hard floor with her back to the corner, going in and out of a stuporous sleep. She had loosely retied her feet and hands.

Wordlessly, the old woman put a small pitcher and plate on the floor. First, she let Sabrina take a drink from the pitcher, then, began stuffing the bread into her mouth, all without really looking at her.

"Where am I" Sabrina asked in Galactic. When no answer was forthcoming, "Who are you?" Looking at the old woman, she realized in all probability she had never heard Galactic spoken before.

When the woman left, Sabrina leaned back into the corner again, her face slack with apathy. She must have been dozing when a while later the door opened and Prince Sarum walked in. He smiled, and his smile took on a malevolent aspect. He swaggered toward her, his hands on his hips. "How is the mighty captain now?" he mocked. "Will you order me around again? Confine me to my quarters? Now you will pay for the embarrassment you have caused me."

Sarum's triumphant malice was unrestrained.

Sabrina's lips tightened into distaste as she silently lay on the floor.

She watched his every move through half closed eyes. The drug had yet to fully wear off. She still felt nauseated, but less so, since she had eaten. Her mind responded sluggishly.

When she didn't answer, he began kicking her viscously. "You will answer when I talk to you. You will kiss my boots if I say so. You will do as I say," he screeched. Bending down, he jerking at her clothes and dragged her up by the back of her collar. When she was standing up, he began to shake her back and forth.

Sabrina looked stoically at him, not making a sound. Then she shuck off the thongs from her wrists and legs. She watched her hand like in a slow motion movie moved up. She had to concentrate to hit him across the face.

He stumbled backward and began to shriek. Two men came running in and he screeched, "Hold the damned bitch. I will teach …" but his last words drowned in incoherent gibberish. Spittle ran down his chin. While his two companions held her, Sarum began to tear at her clothes. When they wouldn't come off, he took a knife and literally hacked them off, stabbing and slashing at her. Then he took a rubber club and began beating her in the face, across her breasts which were full of milk, her thighs and buttocks.

To protect herself, Sabrina rolled into a ball.

Then he raped her. His body heaved from his exertion and his breath came in ragged gasps. With his fury was spent, he ordered his companions to continue. It went on and on. She withdrew much of her awareness from this nightmare. Also, there was a mind searching for her. She perceived a feeling of abandonment and panic. Logan! It seemed like he was behind a door and she had to keep it shut, to keep him out. She must keep what was happening to her from his awareness. Several times, she slipped into unconsciousness only to be revived by a bucket of cold water being thrown on her. When she came too, she had no idea how much time had passed until they had finally left her alone. Her mind was screaming and her nerves were raw. She never thought she could hurt that much and she was shivering from shock and from the loss of blood. She was bleeding from several cuts and stab-wounds.

It took all her willpower to calm herself enough to go into a trance, and her call for help went out to Miri. She must have feinted again because suddenly someone touched her and she flinched.

"Oh my stars! Sabrina what happened? You look awful."

"I guess I do," Sabrina whispered through a swollen mouth.

"Who did this?"

"Never mind. Get me out of here."

"Okay, I'll get the Peregrine, and then beam you up. Sit still. I'll be right back."

To Sabrina it seemed almost instantaneous when the beam enveloped her, and then she was on the Peregrine.

Miri landed the ship at the Space Port.

Chapter 11

Meanwhile on the Araxes, Joran, as soon as Mardel walked in, tried to contact Sabrina. When she didn't answer, he immediately suspected foul play. He contacted police headquarters, but was told that Captain Hennesee had never arrived. When Joran tried to report her missing, he ran into red tape. She had to be missing at least twenty-four hours before they would put out an alert.

Joran's next move was to go to the Acheron embassy. He called and was told that the Ambassador was in.

At the Embassy, he was admitted instantly to the ambassador's office.

"Joran Sandor, what can I do for you?"

Joran's smile was perfunctory as he clasped the ambassador's hand.

"Ambassador Saren, I have a missing captain," he told him with a depreciating smile. He handed Saren a paper with Sabrina's description. He also told him about Mardel's incident, and that Sabrina wasn't answering her communicator.

"And that is not normal behavior from her?"

"No, Ambassador Saren, and there is more," and he told the ambassador about Sarum el Mashad.

"That puts an entirely different light on this. I am familiar with the Mashad family, and they don't have a very good reputation. Prince Sarum was off planet for a considerable time, so I don't know too much about him. I will contact police headquarters, and also the Mashad family. This is all I can do for right now. How is Thalia?"

"Last time I heard, Thalia was on Daugave and Aram on Madras."

Saren rose and extended his hand, "Joran, I will do all I can, and where can I contact you?"

"I am on the Araxes. I will make sure someone is on call. Ambassador, thank you for seeing me so promptly."

Joran return to the Araxes and there was still no word from Sabrina.

Within a short time, police headquarters contacted the Araxes. Mardel took the call and was informed that an alert had gone out to search for Captain Hennesee. And yes, they had a description of her. But when after hours of searching she could not be found within the Space Port complex, Joran became frantic and sent the old Earth SOS out into space.

* * *

Sargon was on the Explorer in the Hyades when he picked up the signal. He contacted the Araxes, and Joran told him about Sabrina's disappearance. Sargon immediately turned command over to Murasaki. Taking Scout I, and using the special effect, landed within minutes on Voran. When he exited the Scout, he raced for the Araxes. The doors to the Araxes stood open and Sargon sped up the steps shouting for Joran.

Also Karsten on the Aurora Borealis had heard the distress signal. He contacted the Explorer and was told by Murasaki that Sabrina was on Voran, and missing.

Using the special effect, the Aurora dropped into real space at the same time Miri was landing in the Peregrine in answer to the SOS. Beaming down to the planet, Karsten arrived right after Miri, who exited her ship using her disappearing trick.

"Hey," Miri called out behind Sargon. "What's going on?" She entered the Araxes right behind Sargon with Karsten at her heels.

When Joran heard the voices he immediately left the cockpit only to run into three figures looming up before him in the hallway.

"Sabrina, we can't find her," Joran told them, agitated.

"Where's Logan?" Sargon wanted to know.

"He's in there, screaming his head off. He hasn't stopped since Sabrina disappeared."

Okay Joran, report," Sargon demanded while walking toward the door he could hear Logan crying behind.

While Sargon tried to soothe his son, Joran told him of the Mardel incident, and then about Prince Sarum el Mashad.

When he finished, Sargon asked, "and you think he had something to do with Sabrina's disappearance?"

"Yes. I'm sure of it."

Sargon went down into a meditative level.

"I can't find her," he said astonished, as he came out of his trance.

"I got her, "Miri suddenly yelled.

She instantly disappeared and within a short time Araxes' screen showed the Peregrine leaving.

* * *

When Miri returned, Sargon and Karsten sped over to the Peregrine.

"Did you find her?" Sargon shouted, as he hurried down Peregrine's corridor.

Miri's face was drawn as she wordlessly pointed to the unconscious Sabrina still lying naked on the transporter pads.

Sabrina's face and eyes were swollen.

The blood drained from Sargon's face when he saw her breasts. They had been beaten while full of milk, and in places it had ruptured the skin. He bent down and immediately began to examine her. First he probed the many stab wounds and bruises while Miri went to get the med-kit. When Sargon pulled her legs apart, he winced when he saw the blood, torn muscles, and black and blue bruises.

"Oh my stars," Karsten said, as he bend over Sabrina to take her pulse. "Sargon, her pulse is weak and she lost a lot of blood. We need to get her on life-support."

Miri returned and handed Sargon her med-kit. "Here is an antibiotic and pain killer, that's all I have here," she told him.

When Sargon administered the injection, Sabrina moaned and a quiver ran though her body. Painfully, she drew air deeply into her lungs. A shudder passed over her swollen face and mouth. She ran the tip of her tongue over her dry lips, but withdrew from the pain it caused. Finally, her teeth unclenched with a long, sighing moan and her eyes snapped open.

"Easy Sabrina, you're all right," Sargon told her.

"Sargon? Miri! Oh God," she moaned and slid back into unconsciousness.

"She has fainted from the tremendous nerve and psychic overload," Karsten said, as he scanned Sabrina.

"I surmised it when I couldn't locate her. She must have had one hell of a wall up to shield Logan."

"Let's beam her up to the Borealis where Teva and Shela can look after her."

Sargon gathered Sabrina up into his arms and Miri beamed him and Karsten over to the Borealis' infirmary. As he laid her down on the bed, she came too.

"Logan?" she asked immediately.

"He's okay. He is with Joran and sleeping right now."

In the mean time, Karsten was busy hooking Sabrina up to the life support system. She was only dimly aware of the activities around her. She felt so tired. Slowly she opened her eyes and saw Sargon sitting on the bed, observing her closely.

"Jim," she said, and reached for him.

He enfolded her in his arms. "You're safe. I'm here," he told her.

"And I'm here too," Karsten said. "And so is Miri."

Sabrina gave Karsten a wane smile.

Karsten sat down on the other side of the bed, and took Sabrina from Sargon's arms. He laid her back on the bed, observing her reflectively.

"What are you trying to do?" Sargon asked.

"Start the healing process by putting Sabrina into a healing trance."

"I will augment you."

Both men slid into a trance and slowly and meticulously went over Sabrina's body, cell by cell. With their mind's power, they energized the damaged cells. Then for a while both watched the monitor above Sabrina's bed, and when it showed improved body function, they left.

Sargon called Teva and asked him to watch the monitor and to notify him if Sabrina tried to come prematurely out of the trance. He and Karsten left and beamed down to the Araxes to see about Logan.

"You are worried about a back-lash from Sabrina's ordeal?" Karsten asked as he tried to keep in step with Sargon.

"Can you imagine the psychological damage to Logan?"

"The terror would have been unbearable."

"Since he is still alive, her shields must have held."

Joran saw Sargon come toward the Araxes and met him with Logan in his arms.

"I'm glad you are here," Joran said, the relief visible on his haggard and drawn faces. "Logan has cried himself into exhaustion. Did you find Sabrina?"

"Miri found her," Sargon told him, and reached for his son. Logan was sleeping, totally exhausted, but still squirming fitfully. Ever so often his mouth would quiver in a sigh. He had been crying since Sabrina put up her shield to protect him from being part of what was happening to her. The only thing Logan understood was that his mother had suddenly disappeared.

Sargon mind-melded with his son and could find no damage. Using his bonding, he enveloped Logan in his love, and reassured him that his mother was there, loved him, and that she was coming back.

A long sigh lifted the baby's chest and his sleep became deeper and more peaceful.

"What happened to her? Where did she disappear too?"

"Joran, Sabrina was abducted and raped; we suspect by Price Sarum."

"Oh God!" Joran took a deep breath and then let it out. His voice was tight when he asked, "Where is she?"

"She is on the Borealis and sleeping.

"I should never have let her go."

Sargon gave him an exasperated look. "To feel guilty about it is senseless. Anyway, she would have gone because she felt obligated. She is the captain," he reminded Joran.

"Where are we going from here?" Karsten asked Sargon.

"First, I'm going to the administration building to get a permit to enter the City. Then I will visit the Chiron embassy to lodge a complaint against the Mashad clan."

"Can I come with you?" Joran asked.

"No Joran. You and Karsten better keep on eye on Sabrina. I'm taking Logan with me. I will use him as the litigant."

"That might work," Joran said, after giving it some thought.

* * *

The permit was granted instantly and Sargon went to the Chiron embassy.

The Chiron ambassador listened to Sargon, then, said, "Captain, the Mashad family is very powerful, but Prince Sarum has definitely fallen out of favor. His mother's family are rivals to the Mashad's. She was given to the Mashad clan to seal a peace agreement. Also, the prince was taken off planet as a hostage to the King. Now, Sarum's father has another son by a younger wife. The prince has lost his importance. I don't know if you will get your grievance redressed by the Mashads, but I will inform his Majesty and their religious leaders. I will launch a protest using the strongest language I can without getting too insulting. It is against their religious tenets to harm a nursing mother."

"When do think you will get a reply?"

"I will have the letter hand carried."

"I appreciate your efforts, and you can reach me via the Port City."

* * *

The reply came sooner then Sargon had expected. He was invited to appear at the Citadel. Joran wanted to come, but Sargon advised against it. He took Logan, to drive home the point that the child was, and still is, deprived of his mother's presence.

The Chiron ambassador was waiting for Sargon in one of the palace anterooms. When he saw Logan, his face registered mild surprise. "Your son?" the ambassador asked.

"Yes."

"This will be interesting. Prince Sarum described someone else as the woman's consort."

Sargon smiled. "I see. The Prince must be referring to Joran, the steward on the Araxes. He is the interstellar lawyer for the merchant House of Sandor. Sometimes he goes on business trips on its behalf."

"I see. When Prince Sarum was questioned he indicated that there was an intimate relationship between the lady and this man."

"Sabrina Hennesee ra Thalon is the Captain of the Araxes, and Joran Sandor the assigned steward on the ship. What seemed intimate to Prince Sarum may only have been a discussion about the ship's business.

"Are you the husband of Sabrina Hennesee?' the ambassador asked.

A wry expression crossed Sargon's face as he parried with, "Do all women on Khitan marry?"

The Chiron women shared equal status with the men and often refuse to bond, but became pregnant through artificial insemination. Bonding meant an intimate and very personal joining beyond the physical. Many men and women were not always willing to enter such a relationship that could only be broken by death.

The ambassador raised an eyebrow and gave Sargon a probing look, then without a comment turned toward the door. "Let's enter. I think everyone should be assembled by now."

As both men walked into the room, Sargon's powerful presence insinuated itself on everyone and all eyes turned toward him. To the consternation of those congregated, he ignored protocol and strode silently up to the conference table and set Logan on it, facing King Mirco. Logan looked up and no one could be mistaken who's son he was. It was unprecedented for the king to be present, but the interest of the Chiron ambassador in this sordid matter, and the strong wording of the brief, had piqued his curiosity.

When the King's eyes met Sargon's, he nearly rose. Unmistakably there was an equal, maybe more than an equal. King Mirko had met potentates before, and also starship captains. He had been one before being recalled to take up the Crown. Because of his wide experiences, and despite his country's backwardness, he had joined the Planetary Alliance and opened part of Voran for a base and trading center.

"Captain Thalon," King Mirko said, having taken his measure.

"Your Majesty," Sargon answered, smiling with a hard tightening of his lips, and a minute inclination of his head.

"We have read the complaint presented by the Chiron Ambassador."

"I am very gratified by your immediate attention to our complaint. I am here on behalf of my sixteen month old son Logan who has been unjustly deprived of his mother, and so suffered at the hand of Price Sarum. I have a medical report signed by a physician regarding the condition of Captain Hennesee, Logan's mother. I also have a statement by Sabrina Hennesee ra Thalon."

Sargon handed the two reports to an attendant waiting at his elbow. The King read both reports. "The perpetration of this action is an outrage," he said, and handed the papers to the religious leader. The King had very little liking for the Mashad clan who had not to long ago tried to overthrow him. This was the reason Prince Sarum had been sent off planet as a hostage. So anything against the Mashads was to his advantage.

Logan had been very cooperative until then, but became fretful. With a plaintive and questioning voice he asked, "Mama? Mama? Mama?" over and over again as he pulled on Sargon's shirt. Sargon picked him up and tried to comfort him.

The religious leader asked Sargon, "You will vouch for the integrity of this woman?"

"Sir, the plaintiff is Logan Hennesee ra Thalon, not his mother. As you can hear, he is very distraught by her absence. Because of the severity of her injuries suffered, she is no longer able to nurse him. And this vile action also caused severe psychological damage to this child."

Suddenly, Logan became excited and tried to crawl over Sargon's shoulder by pulling on his shirt and hair. Logan let out little squeals and bounced up and down on Sargon's chest.

The door opened and Sabrina entered cloaked and dressed Acheron style. She was accompanied by Kendra and Mardel.

Sabrina immediately retrieved her son, then stepped back and slowly sank down against the wall. When Logan couldn't see her face, he peeked under her hood. When this didn't have the desired effect, he pulled the hood off. When it came off, a gasp escaped from everyone sitting at the table. Sabrina's face was swollen and bruised, with one eye sunken into folds of battered flesh.

Logan's pudgy little hand went toward the unrecognizable face and everyone could hear the plaintive question, "Mama?"

Then he began pulling at her clothes, he wanted to be nursed. Sabrina held up a bottle, which he instantly rejected. She took his little face into her hands and bent over him, transmitting that she could no longer nurse him. Logan let out a wail and slapped at the bottle when she offered it again. Sabrina scanned him and detected a willingness to drink from a cup. A servant handed her a cup and she poured the liquid into it, which Logan reluctantly accepted. The child's actions were duly noted by the men at the conference table; especially by the Chiron Ambassador.

He turned to Sargon. "Is this child bonded to his mother?"

"Yes."

"How did she keep the attack from his awareness?"

"I don't know how she did it. The child gave no indication that she was in any distress, but cried constantly because she wasn't there."

"Are you bonded to this child?'

"Yes."

"But not to the mother?"

"No."

"Would you please address this conversation to the throne?" King Mirko asked curtly.

"I'm sorry. As you heard, this sheds a very different light on the whole situation," the Chiron ambassador said.

"How so?"

"The child is bonded to his mother; meaning any harm to her, could have meant death to him. This child not only receives nourishment from her, but his physical and emotional well being depends on his mother. I think you noticed that even before she entered the room, he was aware that she was coming. Any pain or distress happening to his mother, the child will experience to some degree," the Chiron ambassador explained

He only received uncomprehending stares from the assembly, but King Mirko, who had been off planet, did understand. "I see," he said. "She was able to shield the child from knowing what was happening to her?"

"Yes, your Highness," Sargon said. "Prince Sarum can not claim ignorance of other cultures. He not only violated Sabrina Hennesee ra Thalon, but also jeopardized the well being, and even the life of my son."

The Mashad clan was represented by Maher al Mashad, father of Sarum. In the beginning he thought this would only be a small bagatelle. Maybe it would only require a financial compensation, or an apology. To his consternation this was turning into an interstellar incident. He sat pale, and very quietly in his seat, listening to the accusations.

Mardel was called as the next witness to give evidence.

"Commander Mardel, tell us if there was any impropriety in the conduct of Captain Hennesee toward Prince Sarum?" the religious leader asked.

"Sirs," Mardel said, addressing the assembly, Captain Hennesee chose to work the night shift so as not to offend the Prince's sensibility, or customs where women were concerned. She stayed out of his way as much as it was possible in the confinement of the ship. The Araxes is a cargo-ship; some of its space had been converted to accommodate passengers. The living space is somewhat cramped, especially the crew's compartments. The day shift sleeps in the night shift's bed, and visa versa. Any so called intimacy the Prince thought he had observed was only a case of not enough space. No one on the ship will violate the personal or private space of another crew member. There was no impropriety committed by Captain Hennesee. There is no privacy on a ship this size."

"Thank you Commander Mardel" King Mirko said. "Captain Thalon would you and the Ambassador please leave this room, and we will adjourn to debate what we have heard here."

Sargon helped Sabrina to rise from the floor. Looking at her "You got a hell of a shiner," he told her in English.

"Well, I'm not too crazy about it either."

A servant came and asked them to follow him. They were led to a small room where refreshments had been laid out.

"I hope this doesn't mean we're going to have a long stay," Kendra quipped.

The only one who didn't mind, was Logan. He had his mother back, even if there was something not quite right about her. Her presence alone gave him the security he had been missing.

They conversed in low tones while Sabrina, not feeling well, had gone to sleep with Logan in her arms. She was glad that Sargon had not berated her for getting out of sick bay to join them. She had felt Logan's unease and longing for her, and she just had to answer.

About an hour later the servant returned to ask them to follow him, Kendra stayed behind to watch over the sleeping Sabrina and her son.

* * *

The religious leader, called a Khadif, approached Sargon as soon as he, Mardel, and the Chiron Ambassador, reentered the room.

"This bonding, is this a holy thing between a mother and child?" he asked.

"Yes," Sargon said. "It is sanctioned and blessed by the church of my people. When it does not happen between mother and child, the priests perform a ritual to cleanse the mother," Sargon prevaricated.

"I see," the Khadif said and wagged his head back and forth as a sign of understanding. "Then, the child would have been psychologically damaged if he had experienced his mother's …discomfiture?" he asked fastidiously.

"The child was put in dire peril by the action of Prince Sarum," Sargon stated.

"So we came to understand from King Mirko's description."

While the Khadif asked these questions they had been walking slowly toward those assembled around a throne raised on a dais on which the King was sitting.

"Captain Thalon, we extend our sincere apology," King Mirko said. "According to our law, there is compensation for the injuries caused. It is against our law to injure a nursing mother. Since the child is all right now, there can be no death penalty, but there can be a challenge. You have the right to challenge Prince Sarum to a duel in your son's name; that much I can grant you."

Sargon paused, searching the Kings face, then inclined his head, "I will accept," he said, and wondered what bargain had been struck by the Mashad family for such a light penalty.

"We will inform the Mashad family. Tomorrow, in Port City, we will meet at eight in the morning and present the weapons. When the weapon is agreed upon, we will commence with the duel. Is that agreeable to you?"

"Yes, your Majesty." Sargon turned sharply about, and left the audience room without waiting to be dismissed.

Chapter 12

Next morning, punctually at eight, Sargon, Joran, and Mardel presented themselves at the area designated for the duel. At the same time, coming from the City, was King Mirko with a small retinue. At some distance he was followed by Prince Sarum, and his father, Prince Maher el Mashad.

Prince Sarum smirked at Joran, thinking that he was to be his opponent in this duel. When Sargon stepped forward, Sarum's face fell. He conferred in rapid whispers with his father.

Prince Maher stepped up to the King. "You Majesty, there seems to be a mistake. My son understood that the duel would be with the one called Joran Sandor."

"No, Captain Thalon is here in lieu of his son Logan who was the claimant against your son."

Prince Maher el Mashad rejoined his son, and again there was a small conference. After a toned down outburst from the father, Prince Sarum was pushed to the fore.

Sabrina had watched these proceedings unseen by anyone. Now, she walked slowly forward. When everyone's attention became focused on her, she handed Logan to Sargon and said. "The Lady will defend her own honor. Choose your weapon Sarum el Mashad."

A sound of consternation went up. Joran stepped to Sabrina's side. "You can't do this," he protested. "You're injured. Sargon told me you lost a lot of blood. Why are you doing this?"

"Joran, I fight my own battles."

"Thalon, do something!" Joran demanded as he turned to Sargon, hoping to find an ally.

"Joran, I have long ago learned not to interfere in Sabrina's battles."

Prince Sarum's smirk showed visible relieve. Not even in his wildest dreams did he consider Sabrina as an opponent. Also, he hoped for the duel to be called off.

King Mirko came over to Sargon. "Would you like to rescind the challenge and we could induce a monetary find?"

"No, I don't think the Lady would acquiesce."

"What do you suggest?"

"To commence with the duel."

"But she is a woman!"

"I know." When Sargon received a confused stare from the king, he relented and added, using a definition the king could understand, "She is also a warrior."

"A woman?" he replied, disbelieving.

"Watch and see," Sargon told him.

"How is she addressed?"

"She is called Lady Sabrina or Captain Hennesee."

"Lady Sabrina, it is against our custom to duel with a woman," the king informed her.

"Ask Prince Sarum if he'd rather duel Captain Thalon or me?"

"I think the question is moot," his majesty replied. "Have you any preference for a weapon?"

"Let Prince Sarum choose," she answered.

Sabrina watched as Prince Sarum picked through the array of weapons. First, he selected a sword, but then his eyes fell on two quarterstaffs. He grinned viciously as he picked one up and turned to face Sabrina. Little did he know that only Sargon could get under her defenses with a quarterstaff. She had become very proficient at it, because, training her, Sargon had literally beaten the pants off of her, leaving her black and blue.

There was another short conference with Sargon, then, the signal was given for the match to begin.

Sabrina stepped into the ring and leaned carelessly on the staff, while watching Prince Sarum stalk toward her.

He advanced with a big sneer on his face, playing with the staff he held loosely in his hands. When he was within striking distance he twirled it and feigned an attack. Sabrina only stood watching and let him have his fun while she observed his body movements.

Suddenly he lunged, but Sabrina parried him easily. When she saw an opening, she jabbed him in the ribs. He reeled back to catch his breath. Angry, he moved in. Again Sabrina parried his thrusts. When he left another opening for her, she quickly struck him hard on his thighs. He was livid at the ease with which she had deflected his thrusts. He was still too cocky to be afraid of her.

Sabrina knew she had only a limited amount of time before the pain killer she had taken would wear off. She let him play just a little more, before she moved in in earnest. When she did, she battered him unmercifully and in the end was swinging the quarterstaff like a club. He lay on the ground beaten, probably as black and blue underneath his clothes as she was. Taking a deep breath she lowered the staff, then, dropped it. Stepping back, she turned slowly and walked away.

With her peripheral vision she caught a glint in the sun and pivoted backward on her heels, just as a knife flew past. She picked it out of the air, and her next move was to whirl around and throw the knife back at her assailant. Prince Sarum sank to the ground, the knife, quivering in the air, had punctured his chest.

If she had wanted revenge, she had collected it.

Without looking back, Sabrina walked toward Sargon. "Please have me beamed up," she said, reaching for his arm.

"Pain medication wearing off?" he asked.

All she could make was a" mm" sound.

Sargon steadied her in his arm as he activated his communicator, and when Teva answered, asked to be beamed aboard the Borealis.

* * *

The next day Joran went to the Citadel, requesting an audience. After a long wait it was granted and he was ushered into the presence of the king's secretary.

"Sir," Joran addressed him, "our departure has been long delayed by the el Mashad matter. The cost of the long delay, and our Port fees, which we have incurred at no fault of ours, should be compensated by the Mashad family."

"Is this not a matter the captain of your vessel should address?

According to your culture it seems only the women have power." The tone of voice was sarcastic.

"Sir," Joran said evenly, "I am the legal representative of the House of Sandor, and I assure you I am empowered to handle its affairs."

"But you let a woman settle the fight, while you stood back," one of the courtiers said.

"Sir," Joran responded," the Lady Sabrina is a master in the martial arts. I am also a weapon's master in my own right. Prince Sarum would no more have defeated me than the Lady Sabrina."

"We will discuss this matter with his highness el Mashad and contact you to let you know his decision."

Joran was unceremoniously dismissed, but later that afternoon the summons came. He returned to the Citadel and was again received by the king's secretary.

"His Highness, el Mashad, has agreed to pay the costs incurred during your stay at the Space Port," the Secretary said. "As a spoil of the conflict, his highness has also given the two women, Edana and Marlo, and the two children to you." With a wave of his hand, a guard flung the two women at Joran's feet and pushed the two boys toward him.

Bewildered, Joran stared at the boys and then at the women cowering at his feet.

"We assume that the Lady Sabrina would not have much use for women, but we surmise, since you're a man, you know what to do with them. Or do you have to ask Lady Sabrina's permission?"

"Since the Lady is the captain of the ship, I will have to inform her that we have unwanted passengers," came Joran's acidy reply.

Joran felt sorry for the two women, having observed their ill treatment by Prince Sarum. He agreed to take them, but was not too pleased. Having to be polite to them on the ship, had been enough of an ordeal, and he had very little patience with silly women. He liked his arrangement with Sabrina, carrying her name and belonging to her house. She had given him his freedom so he could pursue his own interests. He didn't like the responsibility, or his life, cluttered up with these other women.

Back at the Space Port, he found Sargon and Karsten on the Peregrine, and related the predicament he had landed in. Joran was completely put out when Sargon and Karsten broke up laughing.

"Well," he said miffed, "what am I supposed to do with them?"

Karsten pulled at his earlobe and drawled, "Why don't you take them to your mother's house?"

"I don't mind too much when someone is amused at my expense," Joran said, imitating Karsten's drawl, "but you know as well as I what Lahoma would say to that. Besides, I don't think Sabrina will be very pleased. The women irritated her when they were on the ship."

"Sabrina will probably return with the Araxes; I will take them with me. I think we could find a place and use for them on the Antares," Sargon told him.

"That sounds a lot more feasible than Karsten's advice," Joran remarked, then asked, "How is Sabrina?"

"She is getting better, but she's still under sedation."

"We need to leave here," Joran told him. "If she is still not better, Mardel can pilot the Araxes while Sabrina remains on the Borealis, if that's all right with you."

"It might not be all right with Sabrina," Sargon reminded him. "She's still the captain, and it is her place to relinquish command."

* * *

Sargon was in sick-bay watching the monitor above Sabrina's bed. He had discontinued the sedation some time ago and she was slowly coming to.

She fluttered her eyes. The ceiling above … she was on a ship. The Antares? No, she was on the Borealis. She moved slightly and her eyes fell on Sargon, "Jim?" she said haltingly, and reached for him.

"How are you feeling, Sabrina?" His voice was gentle, but detached, his composure conveying an emotional distancing.

It was like a door had slammed on her. A frown appeared between her brows as she lay back down again. When the memories came back, her eyes began to fill with tears. Slowly, she rose to a sitting position, then, began easing herself off the bed. "Sorry, Sargon," she whispered. "I forgot. Sometimes, I wish I was still young and back on the Antares."

"You haven't answered my question on how you feel?"

"I'll survive …and," she said bruskly, and broke off. No, she didn't want to think about anything, yet.

Sargon studied her. He knew he needed to talk her through this, to press her. Even if it meant provoking her anger.

"Yes," he agreed, "you will survive, but, how do you feel?" he repeated with some urgency.

She looked imploringly at him, wanting to be left alone. No probing; nor having to bare her feelings. She ignored him and went to dress. Only after she snapped her belt on, did she look at him again. "What do you want me to say?"

"Just answer my question," he said in a direct tone.

"How do I feel?" Sabrina shuddered and closed her eyes. She wanted to be left alone. But knowing Sargon, she also knew he would not relent. She was a walking mass of outrage. "You want to know how I'm feeling. I'm feeling lousy. Does that answer your question?" she said belligerently. She turned toward him with a look of barely leashed rage.

She seized his arm and her nails bit into them as her face went gray. Mute, she stared up at him, and then her whole body began to shake. Tears of rage filled her eyes and she began to weep, dry sobs at first, and then with the abandon of a small child. Sargon gently pried her fingers from his arm, then, held her tightly against his chest. As he looked down at her golden hair, he remembered another time when she had lain in his arms, crying like this. She had been fourteen then

Chapter 13

Mardel landed the Araxes on Acheron, while Sabrina, with Logan in her lap, closely watched his performance. He's done well. She would see that he was Araxes' next captain. As siblings, he and Kendra had been close knit, but soon their path would diverge. After Rosana, Kendra was destined to become the next matriarch of the House of Sandor.

When Sabrina disembarked the Araxes, a ghost of a smile touched her face as she saw an air-cab waiting to take her and Logan to the House of Sandor. She knew she would have to face Lahoma and Thalia about Machir Aram. His child should be born by now.

There was a reluctance to return to the house.

* * *

Tomas met her in the entrance-hall with a face that was all gloom, and he wouldn't look at her. Silently, he conducted her toward Lahoma's office.

Frowning, she asked, "What's going on?"

"You'll see," was his curt reply.

When Sabrina entered the office, it appeared the whole household, including Chantar and Sargon, was assembled. She stood at the door. Somewhat intrigued, she slowly entered the room. Her eyes quickly scanned the faces present, freezing, when she encountered Machir Aram. She moved toward Sargon and Chantar, who were standing to the side. Her eyes were literally drawn toward Chantar's abdomen. She was pregnant.

As Sabrina walked toward them, Sargon picked up on Sabrina's erratic emotions and eased himself protectively between the two women to shield Chantar. But Sabrina only handed him Logan.

"Well, you have taken your good time to finally come home," Lahoma said irascibly.

"You mean you've been standing here waiting on me all this time?" was Sabrina's tart rebuttal as she turned around to face her.

There was an imperious lift to her Lahoma's gin. "Don't be insufferable. You're late."

"I agree that I'm late, Madam," Sabrina replied levelly.

With a chill voice, Lahoma said, "You have claimed the right to the male Machir Aram, and there is still the matter of a nameless child to be settled."

"I'm aware. Has he explained why?"

"He did."

"All of it?"

"Yes, all of it."

Sabrina scanned her face, noting its drained and tired appearance. "The only reason I returned to Acheron, is to settle this matter."

"Well," Lahoma said, her voice dry and harsh, as she pointed to Machir Aram standing next to his mother, "What did you decide?"

Sabrina had yet to move fully into the room, but now she walked to its center, and a wide circle formed around her.

Lahoma called, "Aram!"

Sabrina watched as Aram, Machir's father, entered the circle carrying a box.

"Sabrina, you have been wronged, and it needs redress." He took two arms-bands from the box and held them out to her. "It is your right," he told her, but his eyes were on Thalia.

Sabrina's face turned white. She had seen the arm-bands in use at the House of Thoran. She walked toward Aram and took the arm-bands from him, then, put them firmly back into the box. She placed her hands over his and said, "I will not use them because of the love and regard I hold for you and Thalia," and closed the lid. Sabrina turned the whole circumference of the circle until she looked straight at Machir Aram. He stood with his head bowed and his arms hanging down at his sides. Then she faced Thalia and said, "Thalia, I return this male to you, he is your son, he is yours."

Lahoma gave a peremptory cough and Sabrina, looking over her shoulder at her, said firmly, "This is my decision, it stands."

"I accept your decision. Now the child; the mother's name is Anea."

Sabrina turned to the woman.

Anae, clutching a baby to her breast, began to sob, tears streaming down her cheeks. Sabrina gently mind-touched Anea, and felt her deep love for the child.

"Anea, please enter the circle and face me," Sabrina told her.

Anea's steps faltered as she walked into the circle. Her face was stark with fear as she looked up at Sabrina. Her memory, still vivid, recalled the scene at the Space Port. Had it not been for Kendra and Mardel intervening, she was sure Sabrina would have killed Machir Aram. When she heard of Sabrina's return, in near panic she had run to Thalia and begged to protect her daughter.

"Anea, give me the child."

"Please Lady Sabrina, please," Anea pleaded.

Sabrina took the little girl from her, and looking into her face, she could discern some of Thalia features. She held the girl up, turning full circle, "Behold, Melora Hennesee ra Sandor." Then she handed the little girl back to her mother. "She is for you to raise," Sabrina said softly.

"So, now you think you have washed your hands of the House of Sandor," Lahoma said.

"I think my memory will survive here," Sabrina said, eyes resting on Melora.

Thalia walked to Sabrina's side. "Will you come and visit this little one?" she asked, as she smiled lovingly at her granddaughter.

"As long as I am welcome," Sabrina told her, and looked pointedly at Lahoma.

"I wouldn't have it any other way. Since you arrived, it hasn't been dull here. Since we are settling things, what are you going to do with Joran?"

"Joran is his own person. What's going to happen to him will be his own choice."

"Where is he anyway?"

"Didn't Thalon tell you?

"Tell me what?"

He's supposed to be on the Antares trying to figure out what to do with the two women someone gave him."

Lahoma nearly choked. When she came up for air," Sabrina, you're a bad influence on this house," she said, her voice gruff. "Two women?" she asked, barely able to contain her amusement.

"Yes, but he's not too pleased. They're cramping his style.

"He was always an independent one," Lahoma told her.

"So I noticed. My business here is concluded," she told them. Retrieving her son from Sargon, she left Lahoma's office.

Tomas was handing her the cloak when Sargon came toward her and said, "Sabrina, wait."

There had been several talks, but they had only touched the surface of her emotions. She had avoided him as much as possible when they were still on the Borealis. In Lahoma's office he noted that she only controlled herself with difficulty.

Astonished, she turned toward him. He reached for her face, his fingertips gently touching her cheek. "Sabrina, I want your shield down." His voice was a command. When her eyebrow went up, he said," It is necessary."

She handed Logan to Tomas. "Shield him," she told Sargon and relented, but with great trepidation.

Sargon's mind almost reeled with the impact of her anguish and the feeling of shame. He read the enormous violation against her very self, the very depths of her despair. Also there was anger, irrationally aimed at him. He had not been there to protect her.

Chantar felt an emotional echo through her psychic bonding to Sargon and left Lahoma's office. She walked slowly toward them, then, looked searchingly from one to the other.

"Sargon?" she said, questioning.

Sabrina turned toward Chantar, "He hasn't told you?"

"Told me what?"

"That I have been raped, again," Sabrina said, her voice expressionless.

"Oh Sabrina!" Chantar exclaimed and pulled her into her arms. "I'm so sorry."

Tears gathered in Chantar's eyes as she cradled Sabrina's head against her shoulder. Sabrina's composure broke and she too began to weep.

"Let's go to my room."

Chantar put her arm around Sabrina, and led her to her room. They sat down on the couch and Chantar held Sabrina tightly in her arms. Sabrina wept deeply and agonizingly. After she calmed, they talked for a long time. When Sabrina left Chantar's room, she had regained some of her self-control.

She went downstairs in search of Logan and found him in the garden. Lahoma was standing in the middle of the lawn and Sabrina wondered if she would ever look so poised and in command. Her own self-confidence had been badly eroded.

"I hope you two enjoyed each other," Sabrina said more composed then she felt.

Lahoma looked down at Logan playing in the grass and said, "He's a bright boy. He should do well." She took Sabrina's hands into her own and searched her face. She could still see the marks left by the tears. Kendra naturally had reported the whole incident to her. "Something's heal, in time..." Lahoma told her, then, stopped.

Sabrina stared at her, her face pale. She had forgotten about Kendra.

"Anything I say to you would be inadequate," Lahoma continued evenly. "These vicious violations are unforgivable."

There was a long sigh and then a shiver of rage when she said, "He paid."

"You kill him?"

"Yes. But in the killing there was no satisfaction or joy. As she said it, her face grew sad. Then with a downward turn of her mouth she quickly added, "But beating the hell out of him was."

Lahoma gave Sabrina a hard look, remembering how Machir Aram had come home. It had taken a long time for him to heal physically and emotionally.

"I know you want to leave. But come back. You wouldn't deny an old woman the joy of seeing him grow up, would you?" she asked, looking at Logan.

"Lahoma, you're an old fraught."

"I know and you know, but don't tell anyone else."

* * *

Before leaving Acheron, Sabrina went to see Sargon. She found him in Thalia's garden with his nose in a book.

"I hate to disturb you," she opened the conversation.

"Really, since when?" was Sargon's repartee.

"Ah, come on, I'm not that terrible."

"Okay, let's hear first what you want, before I take my judgment back." Sargon tried to search her mind, but she was closed against his intrusion.

"To make it short, I need more time to put myself together, so I need you to take Logan for a while."

"Chantar and I are leaving for the Antares."

"That's no problem."

"How are you going to get back?"

"I have Spitfire at the Space Port."

"You know Logan is very much disturbed. Your presence has been withdrawn from his far too often for him to understand."

"I know. But the way I am right now, I'm no good for him either. I can't be all the way there for him. I must still hide parts of me from him, and he knows. What I want to do is, take Spitfire out into space, and with no one around go through the techniques you taught me to deal with my emotion and memories."

"I will baby-sit if it means you'll be back and functional. When do you want to leave?"

"Now. I have Logan's things packed. I have tried to make him understand that for a while he must stay with you, that I will be gone. He's at Lahoma's, and he's crying. You need to go to him, now. Tell him as often as you can that I will be back."

"Yes Sabrina, I understand. I will take care of him." As Sabrina turned to leave, he added, "My thoughts, and my love, are with you."

Sabrina turned abruptly away, her eyes swimming in tears.

Chapter 14

After getting through the atmosphere and far out into space, Sabrina let the craft tumble. Spitfire had the capability to create an artificial gravity field around its perimeter and could be flown like an airplane in outer-space. Slowly, she regained her composure as she fought for control over the spinning aircraft. After putting Spitfire into a circular trajectory, she sat cross-legged in her seat and drifted into a meditative state. Gingerly, she let her memories rise, then the feelings. She knew she must not allow the attack to defeat her, nor fester. The incident had to be accepted as it happened and for what it was. It had created a thought pattern, a memory, and a feeling. To leave the memory of Prince Sarum, and the rape, in the forefront of her mind, the rape would be continuously happen. She need to put it into the past, robbing it of the power to effect her present, and her future. Also the rage she felt at being powerless, she knew, would be hardest to dissipate.

With her mind she reached inward and she found a comforting presence there. God? she questioned. Thank you for being there, she thought. Then she envisioned a white light washing over her, taking away all the rage and pain.

She sat thus for an eternity, only feeling the white light's cleansing power. In her mind she rose above the memory and feelings, seeing clearly everything for what it was, a dream forgotten, and the forgetting would be as if it had never happened.

"We only remember when we keep a memory alive," a voice said to her. The voice was familiar. It was Sabot, her cowled monk from the Trefayne.

"What are you doing here?"

"First, I'm here to help you. Believe in the vision you just received. All of this is a dream. Let it be a dream. I feel your pain. Give it to me, and I will let it go."

He held out his hands and asked Sabrina to lay all of her grievances in it. When she complied, he closed one hand and pretended it was sand running through his fingers.

"Now, it's all gone," he told her, showing her his empty hands.

Sabrina looked at him with a doubting and lopsided smile. "Now tell me, why you are here?"

"As I told you once before, my appearance here concerns the ovoids. There was a rip in the fabric between your universe and theirs. In their universe, they are harmless. But here, they present a grave threat."

"What are the Altruscans using them for?"

"I don't know yet, so I need your help. This is for you to find out, and I will help whenever I can. Many of the energy patterns have become entangled with animal and human life on different planets. I've been trying to extricate them. But some have enmeshed themselves so deeply they can no longer be disentangled without destroying the animal or human. Also the Altruscans now know where the Antares is…"

"Spitfire," Sabrina erupted.

"Yes. The…what do you call it?"

"Bug."

"Bug? The device you found on Spitfire has given the Orions the coordinates of your world, and the Altruscans obtained the information from them."

"The reason I have come to see you this time is, I have lost one of the enmeshed ones, and I can't find it. I want you to keep a lookout. It could turn up on the Antares. If you need help, envision me and call my name and I will come. And, should you encounter this one, he is a large male. Since they have intermingled with matter, they are no longer a pure energy form. Should it turn back into ovoid form, look for a swirling pattern. Behind it will be a sack that serves as what you would call a heart. It is tactile. Twist and pull it downward, but make sure your hands are covered with something that is not permeable. The fluid from the sack is poisonous to humans. Now I must go. We will be meeting again."

"But how can …" The sentence was left unfinished. Sabot had disappeared and she found herself alone on Spitfire.

A deep shadow passed over her mind as she thought about the ovoids. She didn't want to deal with them after all that had happened. Suddenly, she felt mentally and physically drained and found it impossible to stir against the inertia she felt. She remained immobile, her eyes, unseeing, fixed at the distant stars.

A feint rhythmic pulse invaded her mind and became more persistent. When her eyes fell on the instrument panel, a light blinked three short, three long, three short. After a pause, the sequence began again. At first it didn't register what she was looking at. But suddenly, she knew. It was the old Morse code that Lara, Miri and Sargon used when in trouble. Joran had used it when he couldn't find her to bring Sargon, Miri and Karsten on the scene.

Yanked out of her lethargic state, and suddenly alert, Sabrina took Spitfire out of orbit. Scanning the direction of the incoming signal she noted the time laps and calculated the distance. Using Spitfire's special effects, she arrived instantly, but several miles short of the target.

Spitfire's sensors picked up several ships in the vicinity. Hers being small, did not always register accurately on sensors, and Sabrina counted on being overlooked.

Cautiously she eased closer, using the bulk of the other ships to screen her approach until she was directly under the belly of the lead-vessel. She tied into the ship to ship video and audio. At first, there was only static, then the picture finally cleared and the audio came through. She frowned. She listened closely to the language, then, realized that it was Altruscan, but a different dialect and she put it through her translator.

Someone said, "Sir, our scanners show that she's an alien, not a Cassay. She says that she had been altered so she could infiltrate and was on her way back to Altair to report to the Junta."

"I think she's lying. Put her through the agonizer. See what she will say then."

"But what if she's not lying, I wouldn't want to answer to the Junta."

"Well, we'll tell them that we were conscientiously looking out for their interests."

"If you say so, sir."

Up until now, Sabrina could only see a man's back standing in a room with many curious devices. As he moved to reach for an instrument, Sabrina saw a familiar arm bracelet, and then could see someone strapped into a chair. With a start she recognized Lara.

Before she locked on to Lara, she laid in the course for the Antares.

In the twinkling of an eye, Lara was aboard Spitfire and the ship immediately dropped into free fall.

Lara rose from the floor just as Spitfire went into warp.

"What did you do to your engines?"

"Augmented them."

"Oh, you damned engineers, always tinkering," Lara commented, and clapped Sabrina on the shoulder.

"I'm engaging the special effect. I think you know the drill," Sabrina told her.

Lara smiled, still a little shaky. "I know the drill."

They fell into real space fifty AU from the Antares. Almost instantly, they were hailed.

"Antares, this is Sabrina, permission to dock."

"Antares, acknowledged. Dock at your discretion," Chandi's voice said.

"Well, hello Chandi Hennesee. Have you finally made it? Or are you just baby sitting the bridge?"

"Sabrina, bite your tongue, or I will have you thrown into the brig for insubordination."

"Ah, so you made it, little brother. I'll see you when I get on board."

"Good, come up to the bridge, and I'll give you a big hug."

"You're on."

First the outer doors to the anteroom opened and when it was pressurized, the inner door opened onto the hangar deck.

Sabrina and Lara disembarked and both rode silently up to the bridge. When the door hissed open, Chandi stood in front waiting.

"Hi Sabrina," he said and embraced her. "Uh, you don't smell too good," was his other comment.

"Sorry little brother. When you play hero, you don't always have time to take a bath. Where's Sargon?" She looked around the bridge but only recognized Chandi.

"He's on a training flight and should be back soon."

"Have you met Lara?" she asked him.

"No. But I have heard about you," Chandi said, giving Lara the once over.

"Will I do?" she asked him.

"Only if you are a friend of Sabrina," he told her.

"Well, sort of. She just yanked me out of an uncomfortable situation."

Suddenly, a male voice came over the intercom, "There is a little boy with a soggy diaper wanting his mommy," he said. "He's about two years or so old and has Sargon eyes."

Sabrina surmised that Logan must have felt her presence when she came on board. She hit the button," The child's name is Logan. Send him to the bridge."

When the doors to the lift opened, a little boy propelled out of it, repeating, "mama, mama, mama," over and over again until he saw Sabrina. He let out a squeal and jumped into her arms. Unabashed he let her feel his primal need of her. Almost stunned by his strong emotions, she enfolded him within her arms, letting him feel her love for him.

Her smile was gentle when she looked at Lara and Chandi. "I guess we are both stinkers," she said. "We better leave to take a shower. I'll see you later in the cafeteria," she told Lara.

In the lift, she looked at Logan. "Where are we going to go?" she asked him. "You need a clean diaper and I think Joran might have some at his place. And then, we both could use a shower. I think we better go to Joran's place, don't you think so?"

"Joran," Logan said.

"Ah, I see you can say his name. Say Sargon."

There was a stubborn, "No."

"Say Daddy."

"No … Mommy."

Sabrina surface scanned him. "Oh, I see. You don't want to go to your Daddy. You want to stay with Mommy."

"My Mommy," Logan crooned and gave her a tight hug.

She palmed Joran's door open and stepped into the hall. An inner door slowly opened a crack, then, quickly closed again.

Aha, Sabrina thought, Joran's two women, and grinned.

She looked through the rest of Joran's place for Rorry, but he was nowhere to be found.

In Joran's bedroom, she found a crib for Logan and a dresser.

"Well, at least we can take care of you," she told him. "Let's see what else Joran has here."

She opened his closet doors and to her surprise found half of it filled with her clothes from Acheron, and in drawers, she found more of her clothing items.

Sabrina took a long shower, letting Logan splash and play in the water. After drying off, she donned a floral wrap-a-round, and after dressing Logan, left with him to go to the cafeteria. She was beginning to feel light headed, and couldn't remember when she had last eaten.

The cafeteria was busy and full of young people. Sabrina scanned the faces.

There was not one in the crowd she could identify. She was about to go for the service line when a young man in uniform stopped her.

"Lady, you're out of uniform," he stated, and prevented her from joining the line.

Astonished, she looked down at him. "Uniform of the day," she told him.

"Sorry lady, won't wash. Come back when you're properly dressed."

Sabrina turned and walked slowly from the room. She was beginning to feel feint. Riding the lift up to Joran's apartment, she felt sick to her stomach as she leaned against the wall, clutching Logan to herself.

She tried to palm Joran's door open, but it wouldn't respond to her hand. She tore at it. Then suddenly it opened and she stumbled into the hallway. She had thought to come home, but everything seemed to be out of place. Too many people, too many new faces, too much pain. Unexpectedly, she crumbled unconscious to the floor.

Logan began to pull frantically at her clothes, his wail gradually increasing in loudness and force until it was an undulating scream.

Sargon's mind, as he stepped off the training ship, was immediately assaulted by the scream. He raced toward Joran's apartment and uttered a vicious expletive at the door, it wouldn't budge. Using his mind as an intervening energy, he broke through the electrical pulse locking the door, and bust into the hall. Sabrina lay as she had fallen, with Logan screaming and tugging at her.

Sargon tried to pull Logan off, but the boy wouldn't let go. Also he would not come to him, holding on to his mother with all his might.

Sargon dialed sick bay.

When one of the nurses answered, he said, "This is Captain Thalon, where is Sarah?"

"She is in her office."

"Tell her to come to Joran's apartment, stat, and bring a med-kit."

When Sargon bent down to make mental contact with Sabrina, he received a jolt. Sabrina wasn't there. The personality that was Sabrina was gone. No wonder, Sargon thought, understanding the abject terror he felt exuding from Logan.

Sarah came in at a run, and squatting down, slid a scanner over Sabrina's body. "Sargon, she's dehydrated, she hasn't eaten, and she's pregnant," Sarah told him.

Sargon only stared at her. "Pregnant," he said, stunned

"Yes, about three months or so."

"Damn. I don't want you to tell her, not yet. Let's get an I V drip started to take care of the dehydration, then get some nourishment into her."

Sargon tried to ply Logan's grip from Sabrina, but the baby's wail only increased.

"What's going on?" Sarah asked.

"Sabrina has withdrawn, she's gone. Logan feels it and he's frightened. Help me to get them both into Joran's bed. "

Sarah, with Sargon's help, worked on Sabrina until they had her connected to the saline drip, then both sat quietly, keeping watch over her. Logan had curled up beside his mother's body, and from sheer exhaustion had fallen asleep.

Almost an hour passed before a soft moan escaped Sabrina's throat, then tears began to flow unchecked down her face.

"Cut that crying out," Sarah demanded, "you don't have enough of the wet stuff left in you to waste."

Sabrina's eyes flew open and she looked around. "Sarah?" she asked, disbelievingly.

"Hi, mess," Sarah greeted her. "I tell you, you better stop scaring everybody, and causing me extra work."

"What happened?"

"You tell me. When was the last time you've eaten?"

"I don't know." She tried to move but felt an obstacle. Groping at it with her hand, she realized it was Logan. "Oh my god," she gasped, "did I pass out?"

"Yes, and scared the wits out of Logan, and the rest of us," Sarah told her, and pointed to Sargon.

Sabrina turned her head, "Oh, you're back."

"Apparently."

"Have you talked to Lara yet?"

"I haven't had time to find out that she was on board."

Suddenly, the door opened and Chantar walked in, carrying a tray.

"How did you know I was here?" Sabrina asked, astonished.

"I didn't, until I was ordered via the link to fix you something to eat," then gave Sargon a pointed look.

"Mm, smells good," Sabrina said and ignored the comment as she shifted eagerly into a sitting position.

"You stay put," Chantar commanded over Sabrina's not too vigorous protest and began to feed her spoon by spoon. The soup Chantar had prepared was one of Lahoma's recipes and Sabrina's favorite. She let Chantar tend her, knowing it was useless to protest.

Lying back against the pillow, Sabrina looked at Sargon, "What's with the cafeteria?" she asked. "Do I have to wear rank to get in?"

"Oh," he said, then, chuckled. "Things have changed. When you feel better, I will brief you."

Logan stirred, then, woke. He pulled himself up and looked searchingly into Sabrina's face, then broke into crying.

Bewildered, she looked at Logan, then at Sargon. She drew the baby closer and merged her mind with his. "Oh my god," Sabrina said, reading through his mind, she read the terror and abandonment Logan had felt.

"I'm here baby, I'm here," she told him through the link and cuddled him close.

"Where is Joran?" she asked Sargon.

"He and Rorry should be back tomorrow. You need to sleep," he told her, and when he tried to take Logan, he couldn't pry him loose. He was holding on to his mother with all he had.

"Fix a bottle for him. I think he will go back to sleep," Sabrina told Sargon.

* * *

Sabrina awoke with the baby still sleeping and snuggled close to her. She let out a sigh and closed her eyes again only to become aware of someone standing over her. With a start, her eyes flew open. Much to her relief it was Joran with a worried look on his face.

"Can't you be left alone for only once?" he chided. "What a mess you are."

"Joran my dear, where did you acquire that tone of voice?"

"Well, my mother uses it with frequent success, so I thought I try it on for size," he said as his worried look lightened somewhat. When she tried to get out of bed, he gently pushed her back. "Doctors orders, you are to stay in bed. Rorry will bring your breakfast."

In the mean time Logan had awakened and smiled up at Joran. To Sabrina's astonishment, Logan didn't protest when Joran picked him up.

"I think this guy needs a change and nourishment. You're awfully neglectful my dear."

"Where does that 'my dear' come from of a sudden?" Sabrina quipped, "I don't think I gave you permission to be impertinent."

"You're supposed to be helpless and weak, so you have to take what's dished out."

Just then, Rorry entered with a tray, "Sabrina, are you all right?" he asked, worried.

"Yes Rorry. Since you are here, everything will be better now."

Rorry grinned from ear to ear. "I will take good care of you Sabrina, you will see."

"Yes, I know you will. I'm glad you're back," she added.

Rorry was one of Acheron's hidden ones. Many children were born with deformities due to the radiation and pollution the once patriarchal society inflicted on its people through their greed and power struggles. After many miscarriages, Rorry was the only surviving child of Lahoma's first marriage. He was slightly retarded and had been trained as Joran's valet. When Sabrina had entered his life, Rory cater more and more to her needs. In his way, he had fallen in love with a very gentle Sabrina who always showed him respect, and treated him as a human being, not as an oddity.

Rorry sat at the edge of Sabrina's bed and watched that she ate every morsel of her breakfast. Only then did he remove the tray. Joran entered with Logan trailing him.

"This baby has lost weight," Joran accused her.

"This baby had a very difficult time. But that doesn't mean for you to spoil him, right?" and she looked at Rorry and Joran. "Now, I want to work on the computer terminal, and I won't be hampered by either of your solicitation."

Joran gave her a somewhat angry look. "I wouldn't assume to impede you in anyway. Sargon and Sarah both wanted for you to stay in bed and recuperate. But you do as you wish." Joran stalked out. Sabrina's "I'm sorry," just reached his ear.

Sabrina called down to Logistics and asked for Ayhlean.

"Commander Thalon," came the response over the phone.

"Hi, this is Sabrina. Do you remember the stuff I ordered?"

"Yes, I remember."

"Can I get a robot to finish my place?"

"Sabrina, I'm back logged, so you will have to wait your turn."

"Why are you so gruffy? Have you got a bee in your bonnet?"

"No. I'm busy. You don't always have priority," and to Sabrina's shock, Ayhlean hung up on her.

Sabrina was confused, because when she left the Antares, she and Ayhlean had been on the best of terms. She couldn't understand the brusque response she received. She called Sargon and asked politely if he was available.

When Sargon answered, he asked, "What can I do for you?"

"Brief me," was her short reply.

"It will take some time, but I'll see you as soon as I can."

Sabrina sighed and not for the first time that day. Since she had come back, home didn't seem like home any more. It had become a strange place where she felt like an interloper. To cheer herself up, she went in search of Logan and to the boy's delight, played with him until Sargon came. When Rorry brought Sargon into the nursery, Logan let out a wail.

"What in the world!" Sabrina exclaimed, looking at her son.

"I think," Sargon said, "he's afraid that you will disappear again."

"I guess you're right. No Logan, I'm not going anywhere," she assured the child, but only got a disbelieving stare. She picked him up and sat down with him in her lap, then turned to Sargon.

"Since I came back, I have hit one obstacle after another. I'm not complaining that I don't get priority treatment, but I do hope that you will make things understandable. I'm like Logan, nothing seems as it should be. I came home to a strange world."

For a while, Sargon only studied Sabrina. Knowing this posture, she was expecting a bombshell to drop on her.

"The first change came about, when we took on cadet's to train," Sargon began. "Then, we took in people from a dying world. Like Acheron, they had polluted their world beyond living. We took in as many of the children and young people as possible for the Antares to absorb. Most of the arrangements we had to make were to accommodate this new population. To survive, the children learned to forage. Most of them belonged to gangs and ran wild. They are very uneducated and uncivilized. The youngsters age fourteen and up, are trained as cadets, but not at the Academy. Not yet. They are somewhat unruly and need special discipline. For the younger ones we opened another area. You would call it an orphanage. They are also isolated; they are not yet ready to mix with the general population. The only common area they have access to, is the cafeteria. But we had to institute stringent discipline. We also had to induct a dress code for them to enter the cafeteria. That's why you weren't admitted in your wrap."

"I see," Sabrina said. "How many kids did we take on?"

"About eighty."

"I see. Now, what about Ayhlean?"

"What do you mean?"

"Well, I called her office and got a very gruffy Ayhlean who told me that I couldn't demand priority treatment, what ever that means."

Sargon reached for the phone and called Ayhlean. "I'm with Sabrina at Joran's apartment, and she will get priority treatment. She will get whatever she asks for."

Sabrina could hear an abrupt, "Yes, Sir."

"And I think you should come and visit her," was his other comment to Ayhlean.

"Sargon, what's going on?" Sabrina asked after he hung up.

"She had a run in with Sarah and I think it carried over."

Sabrina grinned. "I knew she had a bee in her bonnet," she told Sargon.

"I think that was Sarah's comment."

"Yes, I remember when she accused me of it."

Sabrina sat back in her chair and contemplated Sargon for a moment. But he was impenetrable as she tried ever so gently to touch his mind. Just like in the good old days, he was closed up like a clam.

Amused, Sabrina suddenly chuckled. "Clamming up like an oyster made me feel right at home."

He had felt Sabrina's tentative touch and gave a hint of a smile, tolerating the intrusion.

"Good, if it helped."

Sabrina's smile soured and took what he said for the warning it was meant. She changed the subject and asked, "Would you like to see the alterations I have planned for my villa?"

Sargon rose and walked over to her terminal and brought up the plans for her villa. He went over them frame by frame.

"You planned well," he finally said. "I see you bypassed the original walls. They're beautiful, but as you suspected, within the colors there is a rhythmic pulsation. It's hypnotic, and mostly children are susceptible to it. I almost suspect a subliminal message."

The nursery cell walls were opalescent. When light fell on them, they sparkled and broke into an array of rainbow colors

"Then you tested them after I left?"

"Yes."

"The walls figured prominently into my decorative scheme. Have you tried to decode the subliminal message by any chance?"

"No. But as you can guess I tried. It only gives me a feeling of unease."

"By the way, who has the cell next to mine?" Sabrina asked.

"It's still empty. Kara is one floor below you, and Meghan one above. Both cells are connected by stairs to yours."

"Oh, they want to stay close to mother," Sabrina said, amused.

Sargon only chuckled as he rose to leave.

"Where are you going?"

"Back to work."

"Wait! Before I forget," Sabrina called after him."

"Yes?"

"Did Karsten tell you we found a bug on Spitfire?"

"Yes, he did. Why?"

"The Altruscans, via the Orions, now know the position of the Antares."

"Karsten and I surmised that. We're checking on everyone who comes on the Antares."

* * *

Later in the day Ayhlean came to visit Sabrina at Joran's apartment. The first thing visible was her head, just barely poking through the door, then, she eased herself in. "Can I come in without getting my head knocked off?" she asked.

"Well, come in and see," Sabrina said, coming toward her with her arms wide. "I'm so glad to see you," she said and hugged her.

"Sorry I was cross, but ever since those kids arrived, it's been bedlam."

"Sargon told me."

"Sabrina, most of them are thugs, even the girls. All of us have to pitch in to police them. They can't be left alone without someone getting mugged or stolen from. Let's get back to what you need for your palace. Most of what you ordered last time is already stowed in your cell. Do you still plan to build your Roman villa?"

"Yes, of course. Most of the walls are up and only the second floor needs to be finished."

"Would you like to come and see my place?"

"Finished the Chinese dragon?"

"Of course."

"Good, I'd like to come and see. I've being cooped up in here too long."

"Sargon said something about you recuperating, but wouldn't say what from?"

"Ayhlean, I'd like to forget it."

"That means you won't tell me."

Sabrina only gave a big sigh. Then changing the subject, "I've seen Chen holding hands with a little girl. Do you have other children?"

"Yes, a girl."

"Husband?"

"No, I ditched him."

"Why? You know, this conversation reminds me of the first time we met."

Ayhlean laughed. "Yes, I remember. I didn't like you very much, then."

I hope that's not a carry over."

"You know it's not. My marriage, if you want to call it that, didn't last long. He accused me of being married more to the Antares than to him; maybe so. Whatever free time I had, was spend with Chen, and I didn't relish catering to a husband. While I was pregnant and after my daughter was born, he began playing around. That was another reason to call it quits.

Suddenly, the phone rang and Sabrina went to pick it up. Sargon asked her to come to deck five, section nine.

She turned to Ayhlean, "What and where is deck five, section nine?"

"That's where the new kids are," Ayhlean told her. "You're getting roped in already."

As Sabrina tried to leave the apartment, there was a howl and a hammering of little fists against the door. Logan had no intention of letting his mother out of sight. She asked Rorry to get the carrying sling. When she arrived at her destination, Sargon's eyebrow rose.

"Your son," Sabrina told him, "was very insistent about coming along."

"I think he's trying to tell you that he doesn't trust you anymore."

"Well," Sabrina said looking at Logan," I can't blame him. What was it you wanted?"

"I need for you to take over my math class. Come, there's just time enough to fill you in," he told her. "I need to leave the Antares. Yoshi will be in command until you feel better."

"You solicitousness is heart warming," she said suspiciously.

Sargon only looked at her, then, began to explain how far the class was into math. "The kids, all boys are fourteen and fifteen. Good luck. I think you can handle it." He gave Logan a pat on the head and left. Sabrina had the feeling that he was leaving before she could protest.

Sabrina sat behind the desk in the class room going over his lesson plans while Logan sat in her lap and tried his hand at writing. Suddenly, the door slammed open and the boys came spilling in, loud and disorderly, jostling each other.

Sabrina put Logan back into the carrier-sling and stood in front of the black board, silently observing them. When she didn't stop their behavior, they slowly began to take notice of her by becoming quiet and eying her. When Logan poked his head over her shoulder, everyone broken into laughter.

"He's kind of cute, isn't he?" she told the class. "Now that I have your attention, please sit down. My name is Hennesee. I'm filling in for Captain Thalon."

There were some uncomprehending stares.

"I was also told that your English has progressed enough for you to understand what I am saying."

Several of the boys turned their backs to her, starting to talk. Two continued the fight they had when they came in. Sabrina made sure Logan was secure in his sling, then, she waded into the crowd. She picked the biggest and loudest of the trouble makers.

"Mister, you will drop and do twenty push ups."

"Go to hell."

"Oh, so you do speak English." Sabrina replied even voiced. Then she kicked his feet out from under him. He landed on his face. When he looked up his nose was dislocated and bleeding. Sabrina squatted down, and taking his nose between her hands, yanked it straight. He let out a howl and slowly began to lift himself off the floor.

"Twenty. Commence counting."

"Go to hell," he muttered again.

"I thought that's what you might say. If I have to tell you again, the count will increase."

He looked at her speculatively sensing that she wouldn't budge; he decided to comply. When he finished, Sabrina looked at the class, "Anyone else?" When no one answered, she said, "That's better."

"Before she could continue, Kara came in.

"I came to collect Logan. Sargon told me that you had to take over his class."

"I don't know if he will go with you."

"Oh, he knows me. Some time ago Sargon brought him to daycare and introduced him to his siblings." Before taking Logan from the sling she asked him," Would you like to come and play with Soraja?" When Sabrina looked at her, Kara explained that Logan had taken a liking to his older sister.

When Logan didn't protest, Sabrina said, "Okay, I guess he can go with you." With Logan safely out of the way, she could now turn her full attention to the class.

"Now everyone sit down. Quietly," she admonished when the chairs began to scrape the floor. "Captain Thalon told me that you are supposed to know your multiplication tables."

First, she called roll and noted where everyone sat. Then she called on them one by one. She never raised her voice. If someone gave a wrong answer, she would repeat the multiplication, then, explain. The pace was fast. After half an hour, she let them come up for a breather. She wrote several math problems on the board for them to do on their own.

Ten minutes before the time was up, Joran appeared at the door. Sabrina looked at him questioningly.

"I'm taking your class to gymnastics."

As she talked with Joran with her back to the class, the boy who's nose she had dislocated came sneaking up from behind. Joran saw him, and quickly knocked his feet out from under him. Again he landed on his face. Though this time he only bloodied his nose.

"Those kids have a propensity for the floor," Sabrina told him.

"You had to do that too?"

"Yes, him. I wonder how long it will be before they become believers," she told Joran, sharply eyeing the class.

There was a noise behind her and Sabrina turned to see. Ensign Jarvis from Ayhlean's office, literally dragged two boys by their collars, and angrily marched into her classroom.

"Joran, where's Sargon?"

"He has left," Joran told him.

"Anyone know where these two belong? They have been truant and getting into places they have no business being."

Sabrina lifted their chins to face her. She recognized Mahab and Assir, the sons of Sarum el Mashad, and gave Joran a quizzical look. "What's going on?" she asked.

"As you know, I haven't been to my apartment, or seen the two women since I brought them aboard. Millicent was roped into instructing them on ship rules and customs. I have given them enough credits to live on, but other wise, I haven't bothered about them."

"I see. You better take your class to the gym, and I'll take care of this problem."

"Thanks, I'll talk to you later."

After Joran and the class trooped off, she turned back to the boys. "Where is your mother?" she asked them, but Mahab, the oldest of the boys, only shrugged his shoulder.

"Where do I find her?"

"She has a shop."

Sabrina looked at Jarvis.

"I think I know what he's talking about. Come along, I'll show you." he told her.

After exiting the lift, Sabrina looked surprised. There was a little shopping center. "Since when?"

"About a year ago, someone thought it would be nice to be able to go shopping. A little village sprang up with a coffee shop, places you can buy produce, odds and ends, and the newest addition is a dress shop.

"That's my mother's place," Mahab blurted out as he pointed to a shop with a mannequin in the window.

As they entered the shop, Edana came toward them. Her face went white when she recognized Sabrina. "I left Joran's place as soon as an apartment over the shop was ready," she said quickly before Sabrina could say anything.

"That's not why I came here."

"The man Joran, he is all yours."

"He is not yours, nor mine to give."

"You sleep in his bed," Edana retorted.

"Have you ever seen him sleep with me?"

"How should I know?"

"I'm sure if it were so, you would know." Sabrina remembered the surreptitious opening and closing of the door. And she still felt embittered when no one came to help Logan, screaming in his distress. "What I came was to tell you is, that your sons are running unsupervised around this ship."

"I have no sons," she said, her face closing down with a stubborn expression.

"What do you mean?" came the harsh question from Sabrina.

"Sarum el Mashad is dead. They said no one here owns anyone. I am free. I have started this shop, it is mine. I will have no memory of Sarum el Mashad."

Sabrina rifled her memory. She understood Edana's hatred for Sarum el Mashad, and accepted her unloving attitude toward her children. Sarum el Mashad had taught his sons disdain for their mother. He had laughed and encouraged them to kick, bite, or pull her hair when she displeased him. On Voran, children belong to their fathers, so Edana had never formed a bond with her sons. She did not love what was not hers. Although understanding it, still, Sabrina could not approve of her abandoning her two boys.

"Since you have learned this much, you also know here children belong to their mothers."

"I don't want them," Edana said firmly, and turned to go toward the back of the shop.

When the younger boy, Assir, began to cry, Mahab hit him.

"Why did you do that?" Sabrina reproved him.

"He's a baby, I don't like when he bawls."

"What are you going to do?" Jarvis, who had remained in the background, asked.

"I guess I'll have to put them in with the rest of the orphans."

Assir began to cry again, and Mahab face became one angry scowl.

"I'll take care of us," he told his brother. "Nobody is going to mistreat us."

"No one is mistreating kids on this ship."

"But we are orphans; there is no one to protect us."

Sabrina studied Mahab for a while, beginning to understand. The boy judged everything here by the standard of the society he had been born into, as his mother did. "Mahab," she said, lifting his face, "when I came on this ship, I was an orphan too, and so was Jarvis. Being an orphan here is not a bad thing." She gave a nod to the boys and turned to Jarvis. "Will you take the boys and see that they're taken care of?"

* * *

Before going back to Joran's place, Sabrina decided to pick up Logan and to visit her nursery cell. The last time she had been there was when she had to quit and leave on the Trefayne. It seemed like ages ago.

The lift stopped at the nursery cell area. Instead of seeing a hallway leading away into the distance, there was a solid wall in front of her.

"Where on Sam's hill did the hallway disappear to?" she muttered to Logan who sat astride her hip, clutching a ball.

There was a passage leading left or right, and she decided to follow the one going to the right, calculating that it was the direction angling toward her cell. At the end of the passage she came to an archway that led into a park. "Well, well, well," she said to Logan who was squirming to be let down. "This is getting to be intriguing."

A graveled path, shaded by young trees, led through a flower strewn meadow. Sabrina followed along as Logan gleefully chased after his ball. They came to a brook with an arched wooden bridge stretching across it.

Logan became very intrigued by the water and was about to jump in when Sabrina grabbed him by the arm, "If you get wet, I'll spank your bum," she told him, shaking her finger at him.

Logan looked at her, and annoyed talked back, shaking his finger at her.

"Little One, don't forget what I told you."

She gave the ball back to him. As they walked on, it soon landed in the water with Logan bouncing in after it. Sabrina grabbed him by the seat of his pants and bent down to retrieve the ball. Just then, Logan thought it would be fun to kick the water with his feet and, so got himself and his mother, wet.

"You're a big stinker," Sabrina scolded him, and gave him a light swat on his bottom.

Logan craned his neck around to look up at her with big sad eyes, and to let her know that she had hurt his feelings, stuck out his bottom lip.

As they came to the end of the park, it narrowed into a hallway. Looking at the wall, she felt disappointed; they were made from the material Sargon used to produce the room dividers. She let out a sad sigh. She had enjoyed the opalescent walls and their beauty. As she walked on farther down, Sabrina found her name above a blue mark and pressed it. The door opened and she stood motionless for a moment in sheer amazement. The sun was shining in here and someone had put in a lawn and laid out a broad avenue with young trees growing along its sides. Holding Logan by the hand she walked toward a pillared entrance. She stopped and admiringly gazed up at it. Slowly she mounted the five steps that lead up to the entrance. The door was open and entering the hall, she walked through it and out into the courtyard.

Someone had started to prepare the ground for planting, and her pool, it just had been poured before she left, had now hardened. She went through the courtyard and out to where her garden was going to be. When her eyes fell on the far right corner, she stopped puzzled. A flight of stairs lead up, and disappeared through her ceiling. Then she remembered Sargon telling her that Meghan had the cell level above her. She let go of Logan's hand and ran up the steps. Before poking her head through the opening, she glanced back to see Logan sitting unmoving and entranced as he looked at a still exposed wall. She recalled her unease about the walls and quickly ran back to pick him up. He seemed remote, and she had to call his name several times before he again focus on her.

Sabrina scanned him, but could only read that he was distracted. Slowly, she mounted the stairs and emerged into an incredibly unkempt and riotous flower garden. Looking at Logan, she told him, "This can only be Meghan's place."

And sure enough Meghan came running toward her.

"Sabrina!" she shouted on top of her voice. When she arrived, she embraced her exuberantly. "Boy, I thought I'd never see you again. Every time you're here, and before I can get to you, you're gone again."

"This time, I think I will be here for a while."

"Are you going to finish your palace now?"

"Yes, As soon as I can."

"Like yesterday."

"You want me to be finished with it already?"

"Yes, and living here. Hello Logan, I haven't seen you for a while" she said, and bent down to pat him on the head.

"You work in the daycare?"

"Yes. Everybody has to be employed," she intoned. "We can't have idle people. Every hand is needed. It was Benjie who said it. Can you believe that?"

"Has he outgrown being your big brother?"

"Yes. It's Lieutenant Hennesee, Sir."

Both laughed and walked toward Meghan's house. It was built to look like an old English cottage, surrounded by a white picket fence. At a distance, the roof seemed to be thatched, but up close, Sabrina could see the plastic material made to look like thatch. Megan's kitchen was old fashioned with a table and bench in a cozy little nook. Shiny copper bottomed pots and pans decorated the walls.

"Would you like some cookies?" Meghan asked Logan. He beamed at her and vigorously nodded his head. "And I have some freshly backed scones," she told Sabrina as she turned to get Logan's cookies.

"Scones and tea, I thought you were Irish?"

"I'm adaptable."

"I never thought being adaptable was such a bad idea. So, tell me what have you been up too since I saw you last?"

"Oh, lots of things. Do you remember how I always wanted to be an actress?"

A flicker of humor lit Sabrina's face for a moment. "Do I?" she said emphatically. How could she forget Meghan's fervent statement some years ago, especially if she wanted to get out of a science class.

"Did I ever mention that I joined Chantar's theatrical group? And not too long ago we were on a tour. We had a four- week engagement on a space station," she said excitedly. "It's been great. And Chantar's really tops. Have you met her yet? And do you know she's going to have a baby?"

They talked for a long time, catching up on their lives over tea and buttered scones, heavily topped with honey.

Suddenly the phone rang.

Meghan answered. "You know that's not fair. I just got a chance to see her for the first time, and you want to spirit her away again. Turning to Sabrina, "Sarah wants to talk to you."

Taking the phone, Sabrina asked, "What's up, Sarah?"

"I need you to sit in on a session. Sargon has asked me to counsel the orphans, mostly the girls. He wants for you to be there to rifle through their files, as he calls it. Also, I prefer not to be by myself with them. Sargon sensed something very odd about them, but didn't have time to follow up on his hunch. So, I need you."

"I'll be there shortly." When she started to pick up Logan, Meghan told her, "Why don't you leave him here. We'll get along fine."

"If you don't mind, it would be better for him."

"We'll have fun together, right Logan?"

Before Sabrina left, she scanned Logan. He didn't mind staying with Meghan, but was feelings apprehensive at her leaving. "I'll be back," Sabrina mind-sent with a feeling of assurance.

Chapter 15

Sabrina found Sarah waiting for her in the hospital area.

"I'm glad you agreed to come," she told Sabrina as they walked down a long corridor toward the ward. "Sargon became uneasy about a certain group of girls. Most of them are between fourteen and sixteen. He sensed that they were afraid of something. I had them once in a group session, but nothing came of it."

"Maybe they're afraid because they're orphans and have no one to protect them." When Sarah gave her a questioning look, Sabrina added, "I am thinking of two boys, Mahab and Assir who were running wild on the Antares, evading capture. They considered themselves orphans and were afraid if captured they'd be mistreated because they had no one to speak up for them."

"No, I don't think it's that. Like I said, I have already talked with them. They are not very cooperative. There is another bunch that's down right hostile. The girls we're seeing today could be pliable if it wasn't for this fear they seem to be exhibiting. Let's go in and see what we can do. "

When Sabrina and Sarah entered the room, the girls were already sitting quietly in a semi-circle.

"Hi, this is Sabrina Hennesee and she will keep me company while we talk. Like I told you the last time, you will get out of these sessions what you put in. I'm here to help you adjust to this new environment, and it's up to you to make it hard or easy."

The girls looked sullen and there was an aura of disbelief. After a half hour of getting no cooperation, Sarah gave up. After the girls left, she asked Sabrina, "Did you get anything?"

"You're right about the fear. It's very strong. Whatever they're afraid of is something so horrifying they can't deal with it. They have blocked it out of their consciousness. There needs to be some deep scanning, and I think only Sargon can do this."

Before Sarah could answer, she was paged. There was an emergency involving two boys who had been fighting and one had stabbed the other.

Speeding off, Sarah called over her shoulder, "Thanks, and I'll tell Sargon when I see him."

* * *

Sabrina just decided to pick up Logan and visit Ayhlean when she was paged. She answered and was instructed to go to deck five, section three.

Some more incorrigibles to take care of she surmised. When she arrived at her destination and the door opened, instead of the class room she had expected, she walked into a meadow.

"Well, well, let's see what adventure this holds," she mumbled as she followed the path before her. Not far along she espied three women. Two young females were crouched in an attack position as they circled an older woman.

"What have we here?" Sabrina asked solicitously in a dulcet voice, walking close, but not too close.

The girls spun around and the woman suddenly broke into a grin.

"Sabrina, I presume," she said.

"Lady, you have me at a disadvantage."

"I'm Karlana."

Sabrina's eyebrows rose in surprise. Sargon's lover she thought and the idea made her lips curl up in amusement.

Karlana was statuesque, as tall as Sargon. A thick braid of glossy blue-black hair, sparsely sprinkled with grey, was hanging down her back, and stray curls blew about her temples in the faint breeze.

Her eyes met Sabrina with a frank look and the impassive austere face was illuminated with a quick sequence of expressions that passed in a flash, thinking, Sabrina has grown nicely. Karlana remembered Sabrina as a fourteen year old girl she and Karsten baby-sat when Sargon had to leave the Antares.

"How is Logan?" Karlana asked.

"He's doing fine." Then pointing to the two girls, "Baby-sitting?" she asked. She remembered the expression Karsten had used when he had let her name slip.

"More like training."

"I was told by Ayhlean's office to report here."

"Sargon wanted you to get acquainted with the setup here."

"I see. I already met some of the boys."

Karlana laughed. "The girls are no better. Let's move along," she told the girls and herded them in front of her.

"What happened?"

"Oh, they thought to waylay me, maybe teach me a lesson. I think the idea was not so much theirs, but the girl who envisions herself their leader. You will see her when we get there."

They walked at a brisk pace along the pathway until they came to a courtyard formed by L-shaped barrack like buildings. Picnic tables arranged under a tree made a nice shady outdoor classroom.

Sabrina counted ten girls. They were a motley group between the ages of fifteen and eighteen. In the foreground stood a squat girl flanked by two others. One was skinny, almost emaciated, with her arms folded across her chest. The other stood mute, but Sabrina sensed a coiling inside, ready to spring. Silently watching was a slip of a girl who stood away from the others as if she didn't belong.

"Are these the females Sargon brought on board?" Sabrina asked Karlana.

"Oh no, these here are only the incorrigible ones," said a familiar voice behind her.

"Kara!" Sabrina exclaimed, surprised.

"Sargon thought Karlana and I could whip these delinquents into a semblance of sapience. Want to help?"

"Well, let's see first what you've got here."

Sabrina turned her attention back to the girls. The one in the foreground held her head high and gave Sabrina a challenging stare and confident grin. She was a large girl with tattoos covering every inch of visible skin, even her face. Sabrina shifted her stance a little to get a better look. Without touching, she inspected the art-work, then, watched the haughty face.

The girl flushed under Sabrina's probing look and stepped forward in a threatening manner. A murmur rose from the rest of the girls, and it almost grew into a growl.

Keeping her voice deliberately even, Sabrina asked, "What's your name?"

She didn't answer.

"Her name is Pina, which in her language means spear," Kara informed her.

"More like a battering ram," Sabrina said, glancing at the girl's squat body. Anger was always telling and Sabrina's aim was to break through her defiance.

Karlana didn't quite understand where Sabrina was leading, but went along, by adding, "And so is her deportment."

"Any intelligence?"

"Maybe some."

Pina listened and a dark scowl formed on her face. Her eyes raked over Sabrina who was dressed Acheron style in a silky light colored material. Pina considered her of small account, a sissified female. She turned scarlet with wrath under Sabrina's taunting look. Her nostrils widened and she stared back at her with a vicious brightness. Her raised hands contracted into claws and reached for Sabrina's throat.

Sabrina caught both of Pina's hands and held them tight. She chortled as she looked down at the girl. "Pina, the main quality of a leader is self-discipline. Discipline necessitates intelligence and an understanding of human nature, but most of all, patience."

Pina wrenched her hands free and quickly stepped back. She gave Sabrina a spiteful look then spat on the ground.

Sabrina pursed her lips thoughtfully. "Thick skull," she told Karlana."

Kara, incensed by Pina's behavior, yanked the girl back and pushed her toward the benches. "I think we will continue with our lesson," she said icily.

Pina suddenly lunched toward Kara and her arm went around Kara's neck. "There will be no more lessons and no more of your foolishness. We want to leave here. We want to be taken back to where we came from," she demanded.

Sabrina looked astonished at Karlana. "Does she have any idea where she is?"

"No. She has no concept of flying; less of space-travel. But she does understand that she is on a ship."

All of a sudden there was a knife at Kara's throat. "You will do as I ask, or I will kill her."

"And what will that get you, Pina?" Sabrina asked, even voiced.

"If you kill her, do you think I will yield to your demands? You must think me very stupid."

Seeing that she wasn't getting anywhere her next demand was, "I want to talk to the Captain of this ship."

"I'm the Captain of this ship. Now turn Kara loose."

"Pina's eyes went big and round, "You must be kidding. You look like a bimbo."

Taken aback, Sabrina asked Karlana, "What's a bimbo?"

"A sissified female."

"Is that…"

"Sabrina, for god's sake, tell her to take the knife from my throat," Kara, pleaded, having been patiently silent.

"Uncomfortable, huh?"

"Very."

"Well Pina, you're in a no win situation. Take the knife away," Sabrina commanded, "and cut out this nonsense."

As Karlana walked up to Pina and took the knife, a soft voice from the back asked, "Is it really true, you are the Captain of this ship?"

Everyone had overlooked the slip of a girl. She had kept herself quietly in the background, observing. Now she moved forward and the girls instantly pulled back, making a passage for her.

Sabrina wondered at their reaction, but her smile was affable as she looked down at the girl's upraised face.

"Yes, I'm the Captain of this ship," Sabrina responded. When she looked into the girl's eyes, Sabrina's mien at once became somber. The eyes looking up at her were not those of a young girl. Suddenly, she sensed danger.

"Everybody, move away!" was the only thing she could shout, when in the twinkling of an eye the girl disintegrated and turned into one of the ovoid monsters.

Screams erupted from the girls and in their haste to get away, they stumbled over each other. Karlana had just time enough to grab for Kara and to push her and Pina out of the way. She turned back to see Sabrina in a crouch, circling the energy pattern. When she tried to come to Sabrina's aid, her shout, "No, Karlana, stay out of the way," stopped her. Sabrina was circling and side stepping, her mind screamed for Sabot as she tried to locate the swirling pattern.

The ovoid began to move in.

There it is, Sabrina thought, and without thinking, thrust her hand into the swirling formation. As Sabot had instructed her, she twisted and pulled down. She had only thought of this Being as energy, but what she felt was not quite as insubstantial. Suddenly, her hand began to burn and she screamed, withdrawing it instantly. She stared at it. The skin bubbled up and to her horror, absorbed the ovoid's fluid. The last thing Sabrina heard was a sharp intake of breath from Karlana.

Karlana tried to catch Sabrina before she hit the ground. To her consternation she was prevented by a restraining arm. When she looked, she let out a gasp. In front of her, an oddly dressed being had materialized with a curious contraption. It made a sucking noise, and the energy pattern disappeared into it.

"Who are you?" she asked, bewildered.

"I'm Sabot," he introduced himself quietly while he squatted down to look at Sabrina, but without touching her. He tut-tuted and shook his head, "I told her not to touch them without protecting her hands." He looked up at Karlana and said, "This is a bad situation," and blocked Karlana's hand before she could touch Sabrina. "Kara," he said, "call the medics and have them bring a portable life-support unit, stat."

"Medic, dire emergency, deck five, section three, bring life support system." She repeated the message three times to make sure it was received.

"Medic, acknowledged," came the reply.

Silent and feeling helpless, they stood around Sabrina's still form as she lay on the grass.

When the medics arrived, Sabot levitated her into the support unit. "No one is to touch her. Now lower her body temperature ten degrees," he ordered. Sabot gently moved one of the medics aside to watch the thermostat. It slowly dropped.

"Karlana, call Sargon to sick bay. Tell him to come immediately," Sabot ordered.

Before Karlana could say anything, he disappeared.

"How did he know our names?" Kara asked astonished.

Karlana only shrugged and activated the communication bracelet to call for Sargon. She turned to Kara, "He also seemed to know Sabrina. Kara, take care of the girls. I'll let you know what's happening." Then she sped away

* * *

Karlana was waiting for Sargon in the reception area.

"What's going on?" Sargon wanted to know.

"Sabrina is on life support."

"Report."

"There was a confrontation. Pina challenged Sabrina and me. When Sabrina identified herself as Captain of this ship, a small insignificant looking girl stepped forward and wanted to know if this was true. When Sabrina acknowledged it, the girl disintegrated and left was an ovoid energy pattern. Sabrina apparently knew what it was and thrust her hand into the center of its body. Suddenly there was a cowled individual with a curious device that sucked up the ovoid. He seemed to know Sabrina and said his name was Sabot. He had us call for the medics to bring a life support unit. When it arrived, he levitated Sabrina into it and ordered the temperature to be lowered ten degrees. Then he disappeared."

Sargon silently digested what Karlana told him.

"Describe the cowled being," Sargon asked.

"He wore a yellow robe with a cowled hood. The only thing visible were his hands. He seemed to know me and Kara. He called us by name."

"Where is he now?"

"I don't know. He named you by name and told us to call you to sick bay before he vanished."

"Thank you, Karlana. Let's see what we find."

* * *

Alone in the room, Sargon stood in front of the unit and looked down at Sabrina. Her face was still and looked eerily translucent. No breath lifted her chest, and her long lashes were lying like shadows on her cheeks. He took a deep breath, knowing he was losing control. He turned away and sat down in the nearest chair, his face buried in his hands. A groan escaped him.

A feather-light hand touched him on the shoulder.

"Sargon, she will live. I could not prevent all the chromosome damage. There will be changes, but I don't know in which direction. We will just have to wait and see."

Sargon lowered his hands and opened his eyes upon the lean figure looming beside him. The high boned and aquiline face looked down, his eyes shining brightly as the studied Sargon without reticence.

Sargon drew a deep breath, "Sabot?"

"I am he. My assignment is to collect the ovoids. There was a rip between your universe and theirs, and some have slipped through. In their universe they are harmless, but here, they are a dire threat. By the way, they call themselves the Mir, and they have a hive consciousness. I have finally located them. Now I'm collecting the strayed units. One, in the shape of a large man, an Altruscan, came to the planet you rescued the children from. It was there I lost him. Sabrina's cry for help brought me here, but not in time to prevent her from becoming contaminated with the ovoids body fluids. I tried to shield the child she is carrying. I have done all I can do for now. Within twenty-four hours, you can begin to raise her temperature."

With that, he disappeared.

* * *

During the next twenty-four hours, there was a constant watch. Everyone came to sit beside her, sometimes in twos and even small groups gathered in the room. After her temperature was elevated to normal, Sabrina continued to lay still, almost lifeless, as in a coma. There were several sleepless nights Sargon, Joran, or Chantar spend at her bedside. Sometimes, Chantar would bring Logan to be near his mother.

It was on the fourth day out of the life-support unit that her color began to improve. She moaned and stirred slightly. Her hand moved restless over the cover.

She turned her head. "Logan?" she muttered.

"He is here Sabrina," Chantar told her, and picked the boy up from her lap and walked over to the bed.

Logan's tawny eyes were round and bright as he looked down at his mother. When Chantar set him down on her bed, he crawled up to her and peered into her face. "Mama?" he asked.

Sabrina lifted her hand and stroked his cheek.

"How are you, Sabrina?" Chantar asked.

"Chan?" she whispered.

"I am here, and so is Logan." Through her mind-link she frantically called for Sargon. Sabrina's eyes began to flutter, but this time she slipped into sleep and not unconsciousness.

Sargon entered the room with Karlana and Soraja in tow.

"Chantar, you shouldn't carry Logan. He's too heavy for you," Karlana chided and took the boy from her.

Chantar was in her last days of pregnancy. After Karlana relieved her of Logan, her hand reached to massage her back. "I know you're right, but he's so distraught and needs to be held."

Sargon took Logan's face in his hand and looking into his eyes. "She will be all right. She is sleeping now," he mind-sent to the toddler.

Logan's response was a deep sigh and his head came to rest on Karlana's shoulder.

Carrying Logan, Karlana took Soraja, who had watched with a somber mien, by the hand. "I'll be at my place." she told Sargon, and left. Lately, Soraja had become her tagalong since Kamila had left her in the care of Sargon when she went to Galatia. Kamila was to have been back in two weeks, but already a month had passed.

Once the door closed behind Karlana, Chantar said teasingly to Sargon, "I seem to be surrounded by all your women."

"But only you are my heart and soul," Sargon told her and lifted her face to kiss her lips.

"Cut that smooching out," came a feeble voice from the bed.

"Oh look who came around, and as sassy as always," Sargon said, as he walked over to the bed and sat down. He looked up at the monitors. Her pulse was still weak, but her heartbeat was steady. There weren't the flutters that had worried him so much. Also, the baby's heartbeat was more consistent.

"Where is Logan?"

"He is with Karlana and Soraja. They just left. You think you could eat something?"

Her head only moved fractionally. She had no appetite. I'm so tired, so tired, she thought as her eyes closed. This time, she fell into a deep, healing sleep.

Chapter 16

Sargon wanted to make a quick check on Sabrina and asked Chantar to stay in the waiting room since she was already in labor. Sitting was too uncomfortable so she followed him into the room.

They found Karsten sitting beside her bed.

"How is she?" Sargon asked.

"Holding her own. She's been sleeping now close to thirty-six hours."

"And the baby?"

"What Baby?" Chantar demanded to know.

"Sabrina is pregnant."

"She's..."

Chantar's comment was cut short as Sabrina began to moan and toss. Karsten became alarmed when the monitors suddenly showed a rapid rise in temperature.

"Quickly, cool her down," Sargon told him.

Karsten lifted Sabrina from her bed, and with Sargon's help carried her into the shower. Karsten held her under cold water, trying to bring her temperature down.

While Karsten was in the shower with Sabrina, Sargon called for the life support system.

"I think we took her off the support unit too soon," Sargon said, holding a bath-towel to dry Sabrina.

Sarah came in with the unit, and looked at Karsten, "I thought she was holding her own."

"Her temperature soared, so we thought it best to put her back in."

Sarah moved close to check Sabrina, but her eyes fell on Chantar "Sargon, you idiot, she's in labor."

"I know."

"Then get the hell out. Karsten and I can take care of things here."

Again, Chantar's body was racked by pain, her contractions were coming close together.

"I think we better leave," Chantar told Sarah, gritting her teeth.

"Yes, I agree." She turned to Sargon, "get the blazes out of here," Sarah scolded. "I think we're capable to take care of Sabrina for once without your help."

"Good, let's go and have this baby," Chantar moaned and pulled at her husband.

* * *

Suddenly, Sabrina's eyes snapped open. "What's going on?" she asked.

"Nothing a rainy day couldn't cure." Karsten teased her.

"You're not funny. What's going on?

Sabrina mind-touched him.

"Now girl, that's not the thing to do," Karsten admonished her.

"Chantar? Chantar was here."

"She's been here off and on. So what's bothering you?"

"Something…" Sabrina extended her senses, first scanning herself and then she reached outward. "She's having her baby," Sabrina suddenly said.

"She went into labor. Sargon is with her."

Assured, Sabrina's eyes closed again and she fell back into sleep.

Karsten checked the gauges and they showed her temperature slightly down. He smiled at her, and not surprised that Sabrina would somehow be in touch with her friend.

* * *

Two days later it was deemed safe for Sabrina to be out of the life support unit since her sleep had been peaceful. Intermittently, she surfaced from her dream world. She dreamt an old dream that came whenever she was under stress. She saw images of a flying horse, her Pegasus, and she would slip into the stories her mother had made up for her when she had been little. It was like going back to a time when she had felt loved and secure. But now, the dream was fading and someone called her back. Reluctantly, she opened her eyes.

"Karsten?"

"I'm here, Sabrina. You were dreaming."

"Pegasus," she muttered.

"What's a Pegasus?" Karsten asked Sargon, who stood behind him.

"In Earth mythology, it was a winged horse." He moved closer, coming into Sabrina's view. "Were you dreaming about your flying horse again?" he asked.

"Yes. And I guess I'm back on the Antares."

"Sorry about having to come back, but I'm glad you dreamt about your flying horse. Those dreams always seemed to make you feel better."

"Where is Logan?"

"Curled up at your feet."

She raised herself up and looked down at the end of her bed. "Poor baby," she said, her voice sad, "He's so little and is having such a hard time."

Logan woke up and seeing his mother looking at him, crawled toward her.

"Mama?" he asked, "Mama?"

"Come here Little One," she said, and pulled him into an embrace.

"Hopefully, from now on you will stay out of trouble," Sargon told her.

To Karsten's amusement, she only gave him a withering look. When she tried to get out of bed, Sargon gently pushed her back. "Where do you think you're going?" he asked her.

"To the bathroom for one."

"Okay, let me help you." As Sargon reached to help, Logan very determinedly pushed him away. "My mama," he warned.

"Having trouble?" Karlana asked, as she entered the room. "I'm glad to see you're back. We've had quite a time with you."

"Well, someone better help me to the bathroom before I spring a leak," Sabrina suggested.

"Maybe you should help her," Sargon said to Karlana. "Logan is determined to keep me away from his mother."

"Okay, let's see if you can stand up," Karlana said as she helped Sabrina out of the bed.

Her legs trembled and she collapsed against Karlana. Shocked, Sabrina looked up into her face. "God, I never felt like this before."

"Do you remember what happened?" Karsten asked her.

Sabrina stood still, her arms around Karlana's neck and thought for a moment. "Oh my God the girl. She turned into one of those ovoids," she uttered, petrified.

"Everything is safe. You killed her. In doing so, you absorbed some of its body fluid. It's poisonous and you have been very sick," Karlana told her.

Sabrina's hand flew to her abdomen. "And the baby?" she asked, looking at Karsten.

"It's going to be all right," he told her.

She looked at Sargon, "How long have you two known that I was pregnant?" she asked him scathingly.

"For some time."

"Why didn't you tell me?"

"You had other troubles," he replied placidly.

"Oh, before I forget, wasn't Chantar having a baby? Did she have her baby yet?"

"Yes, a girl."

"I hope her name is Sirtis." Then slipped into his language and added, "Your Highness."

Sargon was stunned to hear himself addressed in his native tongue. "You," he said. "I have underestimated you, my Dear."

Sabrina only smiled.

"Who is Sirtis?" Karlana wanted to know.

"Sirtis was my mother." He looked back at Sabrina, "I remember now how you got that information. No wonder you had that smug grin on your face. I just thought you skimmed the surface of my mind. I forgot you have a propensity for rifling memories."

"The bathroom, Karlana," Sabrina prompted.

Chapter 17

Sabrina did not regain her strength as fast as Sargon had hoped. One night while Karsten was sitting up with her, Sargon quietly entered the room.

Karsten gave him a questioning look.

Sargon only shook his head and laid a finger to his lips. For a while he watched Sabrina's laborious breathing as she slept.

"Karsten," Sargon said, "you must never tell anyone what I'm about to do, especially Sabrina." He bent over her and put his index finger directly at the center of her forehead, and kept it there for a brief moment. "Now, help me lift her out of the bed and wrap her into a blanket."

"You're going to rejuvenate her?"

Sargon gave him a curious look. "How did you find out?"

"Miri told me. I know she gave you the diagram of the Antares after she walked it. What Miri knows, I know."

"Yes, I should have figured, but she didn't tell me about this chamber. I had to find out about it on my own."

Karsten helped wrap Sabrina into the blanket then watched him leave with his sleeping burden.

Sargon had found this special chamber after he began to refurbish the ship. Walking through most of the ship in an environmental suit, he noted a strange energy emanation coming only from one place. It was a small crystallized chamber. Later, he often wondered what kind of disaster could have caused it to crystallize. When he first investigated, he noticed the instant healing of a cut on his hand. When he stayed in the chamber a while, the fatigue he felt just disappeared. He had used the chamber only once to halt the natural aging process of the original four, as Sabrina and her three companions were called.

* * *

When Sabrina awoke the next morning, she felt energetic and ready to get up, but Karsten was there pushing her back into her pillows.

"Sabrina my dear, you are still under orders to stay in bed."

"But I feel fine," she pleaded.

"That may be, but orders are orders."

"Karsten, you're getting to be a wet blanket."

"I'm not going to fall for your name calling."

The door opened before Sabrina could reply and Kara walked in with a tray of food.

"Is she behaving?" Kara asked Karsten.

"Are you kidding? I'm glad you walked in. I was about to put restraints on her."

"I know, she's an awful patient. Sarah told me."

Sabrina sniffed the air and the aroma from the food awakened her appetite. "Boy am I hungry," she said.

"You think that's a good sign she's getting back to normal?" Karsten asked Kara.

"Why, are you getting tired of baby sitting her?"

"Kara, you're asking a very obvious question. I have better things on my mind than listening to Sabrina snore."

"Don't get insulting Karsten, I…"

"Oh, I see she's back to being her own pesky self," Sargon teased as he entered the room with an arm full of books. "I see a good night's sleep really did you a lot of good. Now, if you eat well, maybe by next week I will let you get back to your routine."

"What do you mean next week?" she erupted. "I want to get back to finish my home."

"Work is already in progress on that. I programmed a robot, and he will finish the second floor. Most of the plumbing and electrical circuits are already laid in, and now he is working on the flooring. Before you get up, everything will be ready for you to start moving in."

"Thanks Sargon. By the way, where's Logan?'

"He's in daycare. He finally could be persuaded to leave you."

She began throwing her covers back.

"What do you think you're going to do?" Sargon asked her.

"I'm going to get Logan."

"No, you're not. You are going to stay in this room. Why do you think I lugged all these books in here? You're going to take time off and take it easy. That's an order."

"Boy, I like it when you get manly and forceful."

"I notice that's she's incorrigible," Karsten chided.

"Karsten, that's an understatement," Sargon told him. "Well, I see you're finished with your food, now lay back and read. I specifically brought these novels for you. I'll take care of Logan."

* * *

Knowing that resting and taking it easy was not in Sabrina's repertoire, so Sargon sent papers from his classes for her to correct. Also Karsten played chess with her.

"You know, you're a pain in the you know what," Karsten told Sabrina."

"Why do you say that?"

"You don't let a poor guy win."

"I didn't think you played just to win."

"I don't?" Karsten asked.

"Nope. You play so I don't get too cranky from being confined to my room."

"I see."

"Karsten?"

"Yes?"

"Would you call what I am now a mutant?"

"Well, it did cause some changes to your chromosomes. What it will lead to, no one knows yet. The only one noticing changes, will be you."

"And the baby?"

"There will be changes there too. By the way, who's Sabot?"

"Why?"

"He was there and took care of the ovoid after you disabled it. It was he who knew what to do. He called for a life-support unit and ordered your temperature to be lowered, after he levitated you into..."

149

"He did what?" Sabrina interrupted.

"You heard. He said he couldn't block all the damage to your chromosomes, but he protected the baby as much as possible. I think you're something akin to me and Miri. There was some splicing done with the ovoid's chromosomes."

"You still don't know if you will mutate into something else?"

"No. Miri and I are an unknown phenomenon. We don't know if there will be a metamorphosis. I have a feeling that we are not all we're going to be. That also goes for Lara. So it seems that you, and your baby, will also have to face an unknown."

"Well, at least we're not the only ones."

"Don't mistakenly compare. You're unique, and I mean it in the real sense. Whatever you are, and whatever you will evolve into, will only apply to you. Your baby might be an entirely different matter. That also goes for Lara. We just have to wait and see."

"I knew you were going to cheer me up."

The door opened and Sargon walked in. "You two look way too serious. Is Sabrina losing the game?" Sargon asked light heartedly.

"No. Karsten just explained that I'm an unknown entity. I'm a mutant."

"Yes, I'm aware of that. I didn't think I would have an easy time with you. Like growing up, and growing old. You had to change into a surprise down the road."

"I get the funny feeling that you are humoring me. Is there something more to it that you're afraid to tell me?"

"Suspicious, isn't she," Sargon said, as he eyed Karsten.

"If she were easy, you wouldn't need me to baby-sit."

Sargon walked up to Sabrina's easy chair and began taking her pulse, then pulled up her eyelid.

"I thought this type of examination went out with the horse and buggy," Sabrina said.

"Old methods are not always obsolete. What I really came here for, was to take you for a walk."

"I knew you were up to something when you started to humor me."

"Do you want to go for a walk, or do you think you are not up to it? We can postpone it for another day?"

"Me, being stuck here. Are you kidding? Let's go."

"Don't you want to get dressed first?"

"Uniform or civilian?"

"Oh, just put on a pretty dress."

"I see, it's going to be a coming-out party. A congratulation to a mutant party."

"I don't go to pity parties," Sargon said, icily.

"Sorry. Wrong foot," Sabrina said, and stuck her tongue out at Sargon.

"You did a bad job raising this one," Karsten told him.

"Can't be blamed for all of it. I didn't get in on the ground floor with her."

"Blaming my parents?" Sabrina asked as she poked her head back though the door.

She dressed hurriedly and when she came back, Sargon led the way with Karsten and her following behind.

Sabrina became curious, because Karsten and Sargon had their mind shields up tight. There wasn't even the tiniest leak. They strolled toward the nursery cell area and followed the winding and twisting passages, until they came to the Queen's chamber. This was the first time Sabrina was seeing it. Here, the beauty of the original walls was not covered and they appeared in their full splendor. The chamber was crowded with what Sabrina guessed to be most of the inhabitants of the Antares. There were many familiar faces, but there were many she'd never seen before. The population had grown since the original four and the sixteen kids they raised.

When they entered, everyone rose and applauded. Sargon led Sabrina to a podium.

"For most of you Sabrina needs no introduction, but we have many newcomers to the Antares. This is Sabrina Mary Hennesee, second in command of our home-world. We are here to celebrate her recovery, and honor her bravery in saving our world. And let me tell you, she hates long speeches, so we will go right to the entertainment. Chantar, the floor is yours."

Chantar stepped forward. "Ladies and Gentlemen, the kids worked out a skit. I think it's supposed to tell us about Sabrina, and I hope it will entertain her. I know it will amuse us."

The skit covered some of the pranks Sabrina pulled as a youngster and she knew Sarah and Ayhlean had a hand in it. It was amusing and most of the crowd loved it. At the end there was a prolonged applause. Then the crowd turned toward Sabrina and applauded her.

When it died down, Chantar said, "I was going to sing a solo, but I think I'll change my mind. Instead, I would like for Sabrina to accompany me on the piano." She turned to the crowd, "She is a beautiful contralto," Chantar told them."

"I love it when you brag on me," Sabrina teasingly told Chantar. "I know you're trying to be kind, but come on!"

"I said, I don't like pity parties," Sargon reminded her. "So move along, and do your thing."

"Yes Sir," Sabrina said, and gave him a mock salute.

Chantar handed Sabrina the sheet music as she sat down at the piano. Long ago Sargon, as one of hobbies, had built it, and put it up in the loft, in the library. He had hoped Sabrina would continue to practice and play her music, but she never did.

Chantar and Sabrina's voices soared. Chantar's reach was an octave higher than a soprano. It mingled beautifully with Sabrina's contralto. There was a hush in the Queen's chamber. After the song, the applause was thunderous.

Suddenly, Kamila stood up. "This is getting too serious for me," she said, and started a rhythmic clapping with her hands.

"Now you're talking," Sarah said audible over the crowd.

The younger kids all streamed to the center of the chamber and started the bunny-hop. Sabrina saw Logan at the tail end, trying to keep up with Soraja, Chen and Davida. The bunny-hop turned into hand clapping and feet stomping. This went on until Sabrina raised her fist. A low surge of voices went up, getting louder and this was kept up until Sabrina's fist dropped. Then there was what seemed to be a deafening silence.

A long time ago, during an exam, when the tensions ran high in the classroom, Sabrina had started the bunny-hop as a release. Sargon had stormed in wanting to know what that infernal noise was all about, but immediately realized the reason for it.

"All right, after all these performances, I think we should go and do the cooks the honor and eat," Karsten announced, his voice loud in the silence.

Sabrina went to retrieve Logan and bumped into Sarah and Davida. Together the went to do the cook all the honor they were able to do.

"Hey you," came Kamila's voice behind her. "How are you feeling?"

"I'm all right," Sabrina told her. "When did you get back?"

"Oh, two days ago. You know, I wish you would stop doing all those stupid things to worry us about."

"You know Sarah, I liked her better when she couldn't speak too much English."

"I know. But she was a pain in the neck then too."

"What are you two doing, ganging up on Kamila again?" Ayhlean asked.

"Hello Logan," Kamila said sweetly, tickling him under his chin.

"Cut that out," Logan demanded.

"Sabrina's kid," Kamila said, sagaciously nodding her head.

"Unmistakably," Ayhlean agreed.

* * *

"Sabrina!" Joran called, having to walk fast to catch up with her. She turned to wait. "I want to talk to you," he said her, as he came even with her. "Are you in a hurry?"

"No, I have time before my shift starts. What is it you want?"

"Can we go somewhere and sit down?"

"The cafeteria, if you like. I haven't had breakfast yet."

After putting her tray down, she sat across from him and raised a questioning eyebrow.

"Your house, it is close to being finished?'

"Yes, there are only a few things I still need to move in. You're coming to my house warming party, aren't you?"

"Yes of course, but that's not what I wanted to talk to you about."

"Well, come to the point."

"Sabrina, this is not easy for me to say, but I still want to belong to your house."

Sheer astonishment registered on Sabrina's face. "Why?" she asked.

153

"You are not bounded to me in any way. I know Marlo has joined you, and you are living together. You have a family of your own now."

"I still want to belong to your house."

"You're stubborn, Joran. On the Antares, it is not necessary to belong to any house. Why?"

"I still love you, you know," Joran said, with his half embarrassed and funny smile. "And there is Logan; he is like my own child. You have been my family for so many years. You don't want an old man having to change his ways?"

"What does Marlo say to all this?"

"She will do what ever makes me happy."

"Have you at least discussed it with her?"

"I have. In her way of trying to please me, she has agreed."

"All right, bring Marlo to the party too."

"She won't come."

"Why?"

"She is still ashamed."

"Because of Sarum?"

"That. And because she was so unceremoniously thrown at you."

"That's silly."

"I know, but she won't budge."

Sabrina shrugged and looked at her time-piece, "I need to go. See you at my party." She picked up her tray to put it into the recycler, then gave Joran a quick wave and left.

* * *

Her palace, as Ayhlean so long ago had teasingly called it, was finished enough to move in. To honor her father's Italian ancestry, she had built it like an old roman villa, planning to use the entire cell. Because of the nursery cell wall's hypnotic effect, she had to modify her original plan.

Now, the building sat center in the octagonal cell shaped open ended like a horseshoe. The atrium was now the central court with a colonnade around the two wings and it contained a pool and fountain, featuring the statue of a small boy. The back of the cell was left free to be eventually developed into a garden. She had also planned a waterfall and a small lake. Only Sabrina and Joran's apartment were finished. The others were still shells.

The day after she moved in, Sabrina noticed three people she had never seen before, getting her house ready. When she approached them, they stopped their work and stood with their heads deferentially bowed. She sensed unease and even fear. Astonished, Sabrina back off not knowing what to do. She gave them a nod, and went down to Kara's to place call Sargon.

Her first question was, "Why are they afraid of me?" after she explained why she called.

"They are slaves," Sargon said.

"Come again."

"You heard me the first time."

"Okay I heard you, now explain."

"I bought them at a slave market."

"Okay," she said again, digesting this. "Now, why are you buying slaves?"

"Why does anyone buy slaves?"

"Sargon," she replied, with a warning tone.

Sargon chuckled, "All right Sabrina. On one of my missions to the Voran system I walked into a slave market. Those three people somehow caught my eye. I sensed their misery and confusion. They did not seem to fit. They looked sophisticated. I don't know how to explain it. I just felt that they didn't belong, so I bought them. I knew you would need a house keeper. Medea and Tomar are a married couple and Lanto, as far as I can make out, qualifies as a gardener. Buying them, was the only way to set them free. Does that help?"

"Well, at least it helps me in knowing how to approach them. I hope you told them that on the Antares there are no slaves. I'll talk to them. It just threw me for a moment. I'll see you later."

"I hope not," was Sargon's retort.

"I love you too."

"What was that all about?" Kara asked.

"Did you hear? I have a couple of slaves."

"You are joking."

"Nope, and I need to go back and talk to them. I don't like anyone being afraid of me, or groveling."

"I thought you loved all that grovel, grovel, bowing, and that yes sir, no sir stuff," was Kara's comeback.

"From you, maybe. But not from scared people."

Kara's reply was throwing a pillow at her.

Kara's place, situated on top of a knoll, looked like a Greek temple with a pillared portico encircling it on all sides. Where Meghan's garden was a riotous wilderness, Kara's was arranged more like a formal garden with a lake at the foot of the knoll.

When Sabrina returned to her house, she called Tomar, Medea and Lantos into her living room. She could sense their apprehension.

"First of all, let me inform you that there are no slaves or bound persons on this ship. You are free. If you want to serve my house, you do so of your free will. My life style is such that I do need caretakers. I would very much appreciate if you would stay."

Sabrina received astonished stares.

Medea cleared her throat. "Lady, we are pleased to serve you," she said. "The way we have been treated here, exceeds all our expectations."

"Medea, you may join my house, but not as slave or servant. You are a free citizen here. Everyone works here according to his or her abilities. If you choose to take care of my house, this will also earn you the respect as a member of my family."

"Lady, we don't know how to thank you," Tomar said.

"Just do a good job," Sabrina told him and walked away. She was embarrassed and angry with Sargon for having people feel less than human. Some day she vowed, to return the favor.

* * *

Finally, the day of Sabrina's open house arrived. The door stood wide to an entrance that was a vast room, dimly lit. The first impression was of deep space and then, Pegasus, with his wings spread wide, flying up from the floor. Everybody stopped, astounded. Many took a step backward. The deep blue floor tiles were cleverly laid to give the impression of three-dimensional space, and flying out of it, was a white stallion.

Sargon was the only one who knew the story of Sabrina's Pegasus. Many years ago, he had seen the glass figurine in Noel's house. Noel explained that after she first read Sabrina the story about Pegasus, she became so enchanted with the magical horse; she had to make up an adventure every night before Sabrina would go to sleep.

"I see you remember," Sabrina said, as she came toward Sargon.

"Yes, I remember. You have chosen this as your house emblem?"

"You like it?"

"It's beautiful."

Sarah just came up to the door and let out a gasp, then a low whistle. "It's one of your drawings, I remember it," and turning to Sargon. "One day, she was bored with your lecture and began drawing this picture. I didn't know then that this was out of mythology. I only thought how clever she was to think of something like this."

"I never gave a boring lecture in my life," Sargon said testily and walked away. Sarah and Sabrina's laughter followed him.

"Let's go in," Sabrina told Sarah. They passed through the entrance hall into the inner court. The still dry pool was at the center of the court, bordered by flower beds. At the far end of the pool stood the statue of a small nude boy with his hands on his hips, arching his back. Everyone who looked at it suspected at once that Logan must have been the model.

While the guests were milling around and helping themselves to the refreshments, Sabrina went in search of Marlo, Joran's consort.

She found Marlo in the garden behind the wing she and Joran occupied. Somewhat listless she picked flowers for the basket she carried.

"Marlo!"

Shocked, Marlo turned and stood motionless, staring up at Sabrina.

"I would count it an honor if you came to my party, Marlo," Sabrina told her.

"But...I can't," Marlo stammered, and hung her head.

"Yes you can. When you choose Joran as your consort, you have also chosen to be part of my family. Marlo, what happened was no fault of yours. How old are you, child?"

"Seventeen," she said so quietly, had Sabrina not known it, she would not have heard.

Sabrina came closer and lifted Marlo's chin. In a quiet and gentle voice Sabrina asked, "What could you have possibly done to have the things that happened turn out differently?"

"Nothing," the girl whispered, her eyes filling with tears as she looked imploringly and uncertain at Sabrina. "Lady, please forgive me. I tried to help your baby when he screamed. Edana wouldn't let me out. She sat in front of the door and I couldn't get to him. Please, believe me …I wanted to help, but she wouldn't let me."

Sabrina could hear the anguish in her voice, and patted her hand. "It's all right, Marlo, I believe you. His father came to take care of him. He is a little boy who had a very hard time. But, he's all right now." Sabrina took the basket from her arm and said, "So now, no more excuses, come to my party,"

Obediently Marlo followed.

Back at the party, Sabrina introduced Marlo to Sargon, Chantar, and then Sarah and Ayhlean. Joran was just coming through the house and stopped, astonished. Then his eyes lit up as he walked toward his consort. He took both her hands in his and lifted them to his lips. Turning to Sabrina he said, "Marlo took my name," he informed her.

Feigning astonishment, "You mean ra Hennesee?" she said.

"Of course. Now she is family."

"Indeed, she is," Sabrina averred, then gave them a wave of her hand as she strolled away.

Midway through the party, Sabrina tapped her glass and asked, "May I have your attention?" When everyone was looking at her, "I like to initiate my pool. Would you solemnly assemble around it while I throw the switch?"

Everyone gathered around. From inside the house, Sabrina turned on the switch. Then with her movie camera, joined the crowd. At first, nothing happened until someone started to giggle and point. The little statue was relieving itself.

Kara put her arm around Sabrina's waist, "Only you would think of a thing like that," she said.

"Well, I thought it would be cute," Sabrina told her.

It was later on when Sabrina began to miss Logan. She sensed that he had left his siblings and was playing alone at the edge of the pool.

She took her camera along and went to look for him. Sure enough, she found him where she knew he would be. Aiming the camera at him, she followed his escapades. He had disposed of his clothes and was enjoying himself, playing in the water. As she watched, he slowly progressed toward the statue. At first, he only watched, then, began to touch and to examine it, especially the little waterspout. Suddenly he looked down at himself. Then, thrusting out his hips, he imitated the statue and relieved himself into the pool. It surprised Sabrina, and she had a heck of a time keeping him from hearing her laughter. When she approached, he only smiled at her sheepishly, and said, "my have a penis."

Sabrina corrected his language and said, "I have a penis."

Logan looked at her from under his long black lashes with his tawny cat eyes, and suddenly she perceived his thoughts, 'what'd you mean? If you had one, I'd seen it,' and he reiterated, "my have a penis."

"I guess you're right, you have one," she agreed to his satisfaction and walked off, laughing.

Before every one left, she asked Sargon and Chantar to stay.

"What's the matter?" he asked

"I have something I think you both would like to see."

Sabrina went to plug her camera into the viewer, only running the last segment of the film.

At first, Sargon's face registered only amusement as he watched Logan's progress in the water and his curious examination of the statue. But when he saw Logan imitating the statue, he threw his head back and just roared. Wiping his eyes, he looked up at Sabrina, "Thanks for sharing," he said. "That was simply delicious. Give me a print?"

"Will do."

Chapter 18

Sabrina came off duty and decided to have a bite in the cafeteria before going home. Logan was with Sargon and he said that he would drop him off later at the daycare. The first thing she saw after entering the cafeteria was Chantar sitting in her favorite corner. After getting her food she walked over to the table."

"I never known you to grace this room," Sabrina said, and sat down with her tray.

"Well, if Mohammed won't come to the mountain…"

"What you mean?"

"You have never come to visit me."

Sabrina looked astonished, then, laughed. "My dear, I don't know where you live. Sargon has always been very secretive about his personal space, and I guess you can gather that he has never invited me to his domicile."

Chantar's eyebrows rose in surprise. "Are you serious? I thought you knew everything about this ship."

"About the ship, yes, but not about Sargon."

"I see. I think we'll have to remedy that. Will you come to my home?"

Sabrina rose with alacrity. "Let's go. Don't have me stand here drooling."

Laughing, Chantar led Sabrina from the cafeteria.

Sargon's place was not located within the nursery cell complex, but what seemed to have been an antechamber to the queen's chamber. It was huge in comparison to the nursery cells. As Sabrina entered, she immediately stepped back, awed by the grandeur of the buildings.

Almost Egyptian, she thought. The palace-complex was built on a gigantic scale.

"Chantar, don't you think this is a little intimidating?" she asked.

Chantar chuckled. "Yes, it took a while for me to get comfortable living here. Come, let me give you a tour."

As they passed through the cell entrance, Chantar pointed to the steps leading down to the inner cell. "Watch and count, seven steps down." When Sabrina gave her a questioning look, Chantar only smiled.

They came to a tree-lined avenue. A pillared walkway, elevated by seven steps, led to the palace which was built with an iridescent material unknown to Sabrina. The portal was flanked by two huge stone-hewn falcons with their wings spread, each perching on a pedestal.

"Impressive," Sabrina conceded.

"The falcons, or the entrance?"

"Both."

"Did you count the seven steps?" Chantar asked.

"Seven, something special?"

"You'll notice as we go in farther."

The entrance which led all the way through to the back exit was rectangular. There where several doors, one, Chantar explained, was to Sargon's study, the other to a huge library. The building also contained several guest suites. Going through to the end of the reception hall, they descended seven stairs on to a pillared passageway which lead to a second structure, the family dwelling of Sargon and Chantar.

Why seven?" Sabrina suddenly asked.

"It is a sacred number: a superstition Sargon explained to me, but he still adhered to it nevertheless."

They entered another rectangular hall with doors leading off on both sides.

Chantar pointed to the first door on the left, "Sargon's apartment," she said. "Mine is through the door on the right."

"You don't live in the same apartment?" Sabrina asked, astonished.

"No. It's not Sargon's custom," Chantar said, her eyes crinkling with suppressed humor. "He told me that married people on your planet shared the same bedroom."

"That's true, but my parents, because of their different style of living and working, had separate bedrooms. My mother was a morning person. She preferred to rise early, but also go to bed early. My father often worked late into the night. So, as not to disturb each other, they slept in different rooms."

"A wise arrangement," Chantar agreed. "Come, let me show you my apartment."

She opened the door and together they entered a spacious room furnished in pastel colors. The furniture here was not as massive as the ones in the House of Sandor, but of a lighter construction. Chantar's bedroom had an airy and open feeling. Glass doors from both rooms opened onto a lawn and a nearby small lake. There where lawn furniture under a huge shade tree.

"Let's sit down. Senta should be here with refreshment presently."

"I'm glad Senta came with you."

"Yes. She didn't want to be left behind. As you know, she is family and we have been together since childhood. She's chosen to come here to keep house for me."

"Hello, Sabrina," Senta said, carrying a tray. "I fixed iced tea like you showed me."

"Thank you Senta, that was very thoughtful of you." Sabrina rose and took the tray to put it down on the table. Then she put her arms around her with a tight hug. After Logan's birth, Senta had helped Tomas to look after her and the baby.

"I'm so happy to see you again," Sabrina told her, smiling brightly.

"Thank you, Sabrina. When Logan is here, I enjoy looking after him."

"Yes, he told me."

"Now you have your tea and a pleasant afternoon together. The kitchen is calling me. There is always work to be done."

Chantar and Sabrina watched as Senta, her hips swinging, walked away.

"What's with her?" Sabrina asked, amused.

"She has found as you would say, a fella. She's in love."

"I see. No wonder. I noticed that little lift to her steps." Sabrina took a sip from her tea then asked, "Are you happy here, Chan?"

"Sometimes I miss the mountains and riding my horse, but then, Sargon takes me home whenever he has time. How about you?"

Sabrina breathed out slowly and her eyes turned away. "I'm fine. I finally have time to just be home."

Chantar heard the undertone in her voice. She understood that it was still hard for Sabrina to think of her as Sargon's wife.

* * *

Sabrina just came from the bridge, and entering her office, saw a message blinking on her answering machine. When she activated it, Sargon's voice said, "Logan is at my place."

She had planned to pick him up on her way home, but now she decided to go home first to rest for a while. Her pregnancy was drawing to a close, and lately, she tired more easily than she liked. At home, she set the alarm for an hour and then fell asleep.

As the alarm went off, Medea entered her bedroom with a tray.

"You haven't eaten, Sabrina." It was an accusation. It had taken some time for Medea to stop calling Sabrina 'my Lady', but now, feeling more like a part of the family, she had taken to mothering her.

Sabrina brushed her hair back and looked with mock exasperation at her. "Medea my dear, you're supposed to be the manager of my household, not my caretaker."

"Sabrina my dear, I have only been with you a short time and have already noticed that if you are left to your own devises you forget to take care of yourself," Medea parried, and set the tray across Sabrina's lap. "Is there something you need for me to do?"

"No. As soon as I have eaten, I'm going to go and pick up Logan."

"Okay, I will be in the kitchen if you need anything."

After she finished eating, Sabrina changed into a sarong with a short blouse, then, made her way to Sargon's place. Upon entering, she could hear no voices, only the chirping of birds. Walking further in, she heard laughter and the high pitched squealing of children. She followed the sound and soon came to the lake.

Sargon, only wearing a sarong, was squatting at the edge of the water, playing with Sirtis. He rose as she approached.

A jolt ran through her. Her eyes moved longingly and lovingly over his golden toned body, her mind going back to the brief time when he had been hers.

"Oh Jim," she said laughing and half in dismay, "I wish you would consider my hormones."

Sargon grinned at her unabashed. "Your hormones are not my problem, dear," he told her. He bent down, and with a sweeping motion of his arms, plucked Sirtis from the water. Sirtis was an exact replica of Sargon. She had his sweeping black eyebrows, the generous mouth, and naturally his eyes. She was now six months old.

When Sirtis saw Sabrina she squealed, and reached for her.

"Hi sweetie," Sabrina said, taking her from Sargon. "I came to pick up Logan," she told him.

"I don't think he's ready to go home yet. He's having a good time."

"Well, I'd like to see him nevertheless."

Sabrina had the distinct feeling that Sargon was brushing her off. Naturally, it was not the thing to do. She was not going to leave, yet, and passed by him to follow a path that wound toward a pavilion built on a knoll.

Chantar, dressed in a bathing-suit came striding toward her. She was beautiful, and for a moment reminded her of Lahoma. Chantar was just as tall and as graceful. Sabrina could feel the delight Sargon radiated at seeing his wife.

Chantar greeted Sabrina with, "Hi, coming to get Logan? I don't think he's ready to go home yet. All of Sargon's brood is here," she said, smiling brightly, and took the squirming Sirtis from her. "Let's walk down to the water and join the others."

"Thank you." Sabrina said.

Suddenly, there was a commotion behind Chantar.

"Sabrina!" Soraja and Chen shouted as they flung their arms around her.

"Boy, your belly is getting big," Soraja said, gently patting it.

"You come to play with us?" Chen wanted to know.

"I'd like to, but you have to ask your Dad."

"Why Dad?" Soraja asked, surprised, but then got the impression Sabrina was teasing.

"Of course she can play with you," Sargon told her, "as long as you keep her out of my hair."

"You two sparing again?" Karsten asked, as he joined the crowd.

"I didn't know you were here," Sabrina said, surprised.

"Do I have to sign in?"

"I might not be such a bad idea," Sabrina said petulantly," No one invites me and I have to crash the party." Suddenly, her eyes widened. Sauntering up the path was a tall, powerful female, tawny colored with a mane cascading down her back. Sabrina sensed more then saw Karsten's amusement to her shocked reaction. When she looked at him, he smiled.

"Your mate?" she inquired. A long time ago Sabrina had sensed that he was bonded. Karsten would have been the only other male she would have considered as a mate for herself.

"Meet Zoe," he introduced.

Both women looked at each other. There was the sense of a powerful presence emanating from this woman. It raised the hackles at the back of Sabrina's neck. She was an equal, and probably could be a formidable opponent.

"Sabrina," Zoe said; it was a statement. "We all came to swim. Will you stay?"

"For a while, until Logan is ready to go home."

Later on, as they both lay stretched out in the grass, Zoe looked over Sabrina then pointed toward Sargon, "Why don't you take that male, if you want him that badly?"

Zoe had read Sabrina's emotions as she watched Sargon exiting the water to join Karsten.

"Because, Chantar is a heart-sister."

"But she is not of your family."

"No. But she is chosen."

"The one you call Jim, he is a powerful male, and so is Karsten."

Sabrina was surprised that Zoe knew the name she used to call Sargon. "Yes, both are desirable, but Karsten is yours," she told her. "He would not choose me."

"I take males, they don't choose me," Zoe said bluntly.

Sabrina laughed. "I take males, but I also like for them to choose me," she added.

"But males have taken you?" pointing to her belly.

"Yes, but the one who did this, is dead."

"I know, Karsten told me. He also told me that you have mutated, and so has the child. I like you, you have courage."

"There will be truce between us?"

"Yes, it is possible, maybe even friendship. Karsten has great regard for you."

Karsten was coming toward them, and eased himself on the ground behind Zoe. Moments ago Zoe had mind-sent him a message that Sabrina was becoming uncomfortable, and that the baby was already in the birthing position.

"Will you quit monitoring me?" Sabrina chided him.

"I haven't," Karsten protested. "It was Zoe. She sent me a message that you were beginning to have slight contractions. I think you better leave Logan with Sargon tonight."

Sargon heard Sabrina's protest and came toward them. Bending down, he placed his hand on her abdomen, monitoring the baby. "I think I'll notify Sarah," he said and rose.

"It's not that urgent. I'm only having slight twinges," Sabrina protested."

Logan became curious when he saw his father bending over his mother, and came out of the water.

"We go home now?" he asked.

"No Logan," Sargon told him. "You need to stay here with me tonight. Mommy is having her baby and she's got to go and see Sarah." Turning to Karsten, "Will you take her down to sick bay?"

"I don't have to baby-sit her, though?"

"No, I don't think so. This time, I hope she'll do the simple thing and just have a normal delivery."

Karsten accompanied Sabrina into the lift. Going down, she suddenly gasped. "Stop the lift, I think I'm having this baby," she said dumbfounded.

"No you don't," Karsten protested, "you will wait until Sarah gets here."

"No, I don't think so."

Sabrina grimaced at him as she squatted down. The baby had already crowned and the head was sliding out into her hands. The baby's eyes were open and green, not quite Sabrina's green, and emanating from an open mouth was a loud and protesting wail. Karsten had just time enough to reach for it, as the shoulders twisted, and the child was born.

"Can't you do anything the normal way?" Karsten complained.

"Why didn't you tell him not to be in such a hurry." Taking the little boy from Karsten, she cradled him in her arm.

When the lift doors opened, Sargon and Sarah stood waiting for her. Sarah was about to take the baby when Sargon intervened.

"Have you bonded with him," he asked.

"No. Why?"

"Bond with him," Sargon told her.

"He's not like Logan," Sabrina protested.

"You don't know. Bond."

Sabrina did as she was commanded. "Little One," her mind questioned. There was a slight response. The eyes opened and he looked up at her, then, gave a satisfied sigh. His eyelids fluttered as he drifted into sleep.

"His name is Jason," she told them after Sarah took the baby and wrapped him into a blanket while Sabrina was hoisted onto a gurney and an orderly wheeled her away.

When Sargon and Karsten tried to follow, Sarah waved them away. She was in command here, and she took over.

Chapter 19

To nurse Jason, Sabrina used one of the smaller briefing rooms for privacy. Earlier, the bridge monitor had registered an energy fluctuation. Something was pushing against the Antares. She had her computer tied into engineering and was working on identifying its origin. Logan sat on top of the table trying to open a puzzle ball that had candy hidden inside. Jason slept now soundly in the hammock sling. Suddenly, the doors slid open and Sargon stood framed in the door. He was accompanied by several individuals, all males.

Logan let out a squeal and ran into his father's arms, proffering the ball.

Sargon laughed. "If I open the ball, the candy will be mine. But if you solve the puzzle, it is yours," he told his son.

Logan snatched the ball back and plopped down on the table again, giving his father an aggrieved look.

"I need a couple of minutes and then you can have the room." Sabrina told him as she switched to visual. "Chandi, I'll have a print-out coming through. Give it to Emma to check it out."

"Yes Sir," Chandi replied.

Unexpectedly, the normal hum of Antares' engines intensified, growing deeper. Sabrina tapped the keyboard to bring up the engines diagram. The numbers were constantly readjusting. Something tried to move in on the Antares' position. The Antares was currently stationary in a Lagrangian point close to the Pleiades.

"Engineering, compensate," Sabrina ordered. Still, the numbered readings continued to change. "Compensate," she ordered again, after more fluctuation. "Ian to engineering. Now! Damn it, Lira!" she yelled at Ian's relief, "compensate, then again, "compensate." Looking at Sargon, "To the bridge" she ordered. "Benjie, to the bridge. Joran, to the briefing room."

Sargon left the chair running, as Sabrina split the viewing screen between engineering and the bridge. "Activate all scanners and send visuals down here." An energy field was obscuring the star patterns.

As soon as she saw Sargon on the bridge she said, "Sargon, take science station. Give information as it comes in. Ian, compensate again. I think this is an interspace displacement. I think there's a ship coming in."

"Sabrina, permission to come on board?"

"Miri! Permission, granted. Where on Sam's hill are you coming from?"

"Tell you when I see you, fair?" Miri came walking through the wall, as horrified gasps escaped from Sargon's visitors. Sabrina had forgotten all about them.

"Sargon, any readings?"

"No life readings."

"Miri, could you do your thing and wander over there?"

"Okeydoke."

"Miri, I think you keep bad company, where did you pick that up?"

"Dunno, see you later alligator." She waved at Sabrina, ignoring the men in the room, and disappeared.

"Sabrina we have an emergency call from Acheron. There is a ship interfering with the moon's orbit. They're beginning to experience gravitational problems." Sargon told her.

Joran walked in.

"Take the kids for me. Then come back and take care of Sargon's guests until he is free."

There was still no word from Miri so she decided to contact her. "Sargon, I'm going down levels to contact Miri. Mind the store in the meantime."

"Okeydoke."

"Funny."

Sabrina lowered her mind-shield and went down deeper and deeper into meditation level. Finally she heard Miri's voice in her head saying,

"Hi, kiddo. This is a completely automated ship and I think its purpose is to grind up asteroids and small planetoids. So, go ahead and sent your android over."

Sabrina came back to normal awareness. "Sargon, we have an asteroid muncher. Tell Acheron we'll take care of it. Ian, have Android Three readied and sent him over to the ship to disengage its computer and engines. And Ian, program the android to switch polarity when he gets over there."

"Got you, Lass."

"This is Karsten. Oh, hi Sabrina. You know, I would like to arrange a date with you sometime under less strenuous circumstances."

"Well you seem to have a nose for trouble."

"I know. Excitement follows me where ever I go. What is it you want me to do?"

"After I give the signal, use your tractor beam and push that thing away from Acheron's moon before it commences to munch it up."

"We have an asteroid muncher? How cute. I'll do what I can."

"Android Three, this is Sabrina, give me visual."

The interior of the ship came on view as the Android turned on its axis. It looked like a small control center.

"Android, switch polarity, then, deactivate all control terminals." Suddenly, there were sparks flying all around the android, but because of the polarity reversal, the energy ricochet off of him, and inverted back to its source. The damage to the ships control-room was phenomenal. Astonished gasps were heard all around, but Sabrina steadily ignored the visitors. She had finally placed them. They were from the Voran system.

"Ian, beam the android back aboard."

"Aye, Lass."

"Ian, it's yes Captain."

"Yes, Sir."

"Karsten."

"Yes, Captain," he said, teasing.

"Push it away, and Karsten, don't try to be funny."

"As you say."

The Aurora's tractor beam locked on, and the strange ship slowly moved farther out into space.

"Sargon, I will replace you on the bridge so you can entertain your visitors." Sabrina left the briefing room without a glance at the strangers. She had to wait for the turbo lift and met Sargon as he exited. "You still want me to monitor?"

"Yes, I think it would be best if you stayed with me," she told him.

On the bridge she displaced Chandi from the con. "Keep the sensors on their widest scan and magnitude. I don't think we're through yet."

"You expect some more excitement?" Benjie asked from the science center.

"You can bet your boots. Keep Antares' polarity positive to repel" she told Chandi who took his seat at the navigation console. And she was right. Suddenly a ship popped into view, and commenced firing on the Antares with some kind of energy photons. It ceased as soon as they realized that their photons somehow impacted back onto their hull.

"Emma, raise communications if that's possible."

"Aye, Captain." Emma's expert fingers played over her keyboard. "I get no reply," she told Sabrina.

"Benjie, analyze any energy readings you get from that ship."

"I'm already doing that. Sabrina?"

"What?"

"I think they are using high frequency radio waves."

"Boost amplitude."

"Going up scale."

"Sargon, I think you need to take over the science station."

"I'm on my way."

"You don't think I can handle this?" Benjie asked, his hurt feelings in his voice.

"Benjie, this is not to hurt your feelings. I want Sargon up here because I'm out of my ken. This is not something simple. This is something I never ran into. Sargon has wider experiences than I have."

"Oh, you finally acknowledge that I'm the Master," Sargon said, coming onto the bridge.

"Master my eye, only that you're older than me."

"I had to stick my foot into that." Sargon chuckled, as he dislodged Benjie from the seat. "What have you got so far, Benjie?"

"This is some kind of radio frequency I've never ran into," he said, his arms draped across Sargon's shoulders.

"Let's see what I can get." Sargon worked for a while. Then, he sent a burst of high velocity waves toward the ship. They received an answer back, but nothing decipherable. "Sabrina, is Miri still around? If so, ask her to take another walk," he said.

Emma contacted the Aurora. "Miri said she heard you, and she's going to take a walk."

After a few minutes Miri appeared on the bridge of the Antares. "Boy, those are funny creatures. All brains and no body; at least, not much of one. I told them to cease firing and to leave this Solar system. They came from the same place as the Dravidians, but are nothing like them. They said they mine the asteroids for their minerals and ores. So I told them that their mining ship had inadvertently picked a moon belonging to an inhabited planet. They didn't think the readings they picked up belonged to any sentient beings. I tried to inform them otherwise. I explained that what goes as sentient in their neck of the woods may not be the same everywhere else. They said that they will consider what I have said, and if it had merit, they might even comply. What do you say to so much arrogance?" she asked Sargon, her eyebrows arching upwards.

Moments later there was a sensor scan of the Antares from the ship, and a minute later, Karsten reported that he also had been scanned. As suddenly as the ship appeared, it disappeared, taking the damaged mining ship with them.

"Well I hope that was the last unauthorized visit from that solar system. Those people are not quite as sophisticated or evolved as they'd like to think," Sabrina muttered angrily. The Dravidians had not in the least impressed her with their radiation contamination. "Making themselves out as gods! These people seem to have an exaggerated image of themselves."

"Are you finished muttering to yourself?" Sargon asked. "If you are, you have the Antares. I will be leaving soon."

"What are you doing with those men from the Voran system?"

"They are interested in a joint enterprise."

"Business for the Antares?"

"One of us has to earn money."

"Just see to that you don't get gypped."

"That's why I'll take Joran along."

"I see."

"Sabrina, you have command."

"Sargon, I have command."